"Everyone is here," Max said. "Who are we—"

"I apologize for the delay. I got turned around on my way back from the car."

Max snapped his attention in the direction of the familiar voice. He hadn't heard that voice in more than a decade, but he could never, *ever* forget it. His mouth went dry, and his heart thudded so loudly inside his chest he was sure his sister, seated beside him, could hear it.

"Peaches?" He scanned the dark eyes that stared back at him through narrowed slits.

"It's *Quinn*." She was gorgeous, despite the slight flare of her nostrils and the stiff smile that barely revealed her dimples. "Hello, Max."

The *good to see you* was notably absent. But what should he expect? It was his fault they hadn't parted on the best of terms.

What on earth was Quinn Bazemore—his ex—doing here?

* * *

A Reunion of Rivals by Reese Ryan is part of The Bourbon Brothers series.

Dear Reader,

Welcome back to the fictional town of Magnolia Lake, Tennessee, where my Bourbon Brothers series is set. This series follows the romantic adventures of the Abbott siblings—four of whom help run the world-renowned King's Finest Distillery.

In *A Reunion of Rivals*, Max Abbott comes face-to-face with his biggest regret when he is paired with Quinn Bazemore to promote the latest offering from King's Finest Distillery. The delicious peach brandy is made from fruit grown on Quinn's grandfather's farm. The secret exes have very different agendas, but to achieve them they must work together. As they get reacquainted, things heat up. But will Quinn's rules and Max's sibling rivalry derail their second chance at love?

Thank you for joining me for the passion, secrets and drama of my Bourbon Brothers series. If you have a question or comment about this series or others, visit reeseryan.com/desirereaders to drop me a line. While you're there, be sure to join my VIP Readers newsletter list for series news, reader giveaways and more.

Until our next adventure,

Reese Ryan

REESE RYAN

———

A REUNION OF RIVALS

HARLEQUIN®
DESIRE™

Recycling programs
for this product may
not exist in your area.

ISBN-13: 978-1-335-20921-4

A Reunion of Rivals

Copyright © 2020 by Roxanne Ravenel

This edition published by arrangement with Harlequin Books S.A.

For questions and comments about the quality of this book, please contact us at CustomerService@Harlequin.com.

Harlequin Enterprises ULC
22 Adelaide St. West, 40th Floor
Toronto, Ontario M5H 4E3, Canada
www.Harlequin.com

Printed in U.S.A.

Reese Ryan writes sexy, emotional love stories served with a heaping side of family drama.

Reese is a native Ohioan with deep Tennessee roots. She endured many long, hot car trips to family reunions in Memphis via a tiny clown car loaded with cousins.

Connect with her on Instagram, Facebook, Twitter or at reeseryan.com.

Join her VIP Readers Lounge at bit.ly/VIPReadersLounge.

Books by Reese Ryan

Harlequin Desire

The Bourbon Brothers

Savannah's Secret
The Billionaire's Legacy
Engaging the Enemy
A Reunion of Rivals

Dynasties: Secrets of the A-List

Seduced by Second Chances

Texas Cattleman's Club: Inheritance

Secret Heir Seduction

Visit her Author Profile page at Harlequin.com, or reeseryan.com, for more titles.

You can find Reese Ryan on Facebook, along with other Harlequin Desire authors, at Facebook.com/harlequindesireauthors!

To the amazing readers in the
Reese Ryan VIP Readers Lounge on Facebook:
thank you for your continued support.
I appreciate you all so much.

To Jennifer Copeland:
thank you for recommending
the perfect Robert Frost poem.

To readers Cassandra Hunt,
Nalria Wisdom Gaddy, Julie Eichelberger-Ford
and Nicole Trudeau Westmoreland: thank you
for the peach drink recommendations.
I can't wait to try all of them.

One

Max Abbott had a king-size headache and a serious case of jet lag. After spending seven days in Vegas on a business trip that ended with the three-day-long bachelor party of a college friend, he was grateful to be back in Magnolia Lake—his small Tennessee hometown nestled in the Smoky Mountains.

He'd drunk way too much and slept far too little. And this morning, his thirtysomething body was clearly protesting his twentysomething antics over the weekend.

Max was the marketing VP of King's Finest, his family's world-renowned distillery. So he usually made a point of arriving in the office ahead of his team. But today he was so exhausted he could barely see straight. If it hadn't been for his father—Duke Abbott, the company CEO—calling an emergency meeting this morning, he would've stayed home and slept it off.

Instead, he lumbered into the office still wearing his Saint Laurent shades at ten thirty—half an hour before the scheduled meeting. Just enough time to check in with his assistant.

"Good morning, chief." Molly Halloran glanced up from typing furiously on her keyboard.

He removed his shades, squinting at the light pouring in from the nearby windows.

"Sheesh!" she exclaimed in a voice reminiscent of Lucille Ball's in *I Love Lucy.* "Must've been *some* weekend."

"It was." Max parked his butt in the chair in front of Molly's desk, not willing to expend the additional energy to take the dozen or so steps to his office. "And good morning to you, too, sunshine."

"Can I get you some coffee? You're going to need it if you don't want to look like the stiff in *Weekend at Bernie's* the rest of the day." She bounced out of her seat and moved toward the coffeemaker before he'd even grunted his response.

Molly's brutal honesty was one of the reasons he valued her so much. And if it caught him in the chin with a right hook every now and again, so be it.

He pulled out his phone and checked his text messages and email to see if anything pressing required his attention.

There was nothing that couldn't wait until he was fully conscious, which, at this rate, might be in a day or two.

Max thanked Molly when she handed him a black mug engraved with the white King's Finest Distillery logo. He set his phone on her desk and wrapped his hands around the warm cup, inhaled the fragrant black liquid and took his first sip of coffee of the day. He released a small, contented sigh, his eyes drifting closed momentarily.

"We've got twenty minutes to go over everything." She tapped on the fitness wearable on her wrist. "That takes into account the five minutes you'll need to walk to the conference room."

Brutally honest and extremely efficient.

"Fine." He took another swig of coffee, set his mug down and opened the notes app on his phone. "Shoot."

"Your father is being tight-lipped about this meeting." She lowered her voice, her blue-gray eyes shifting away from him. "But last week, while you were gone, he asked me and Emily to compile everything you and Zora had on your proposal to add fruit brandies to the KFD lineup."

That woke him up more than the bulletproof coffee had.

Three years ago, his grandfather, Joseph Abbott, the founder of King's Finest Distillery, had proposed that the company begin making fruit brandy. His father had been opposed. In a compromise, they'd spent a small mint to set up separate stills and bring in a brandy distiller. The company began experimenting with making small batches of fruit brandy, using the excess, overly ripe fruit supplied by his grandfather's best friend, who owned an orchard just outside of Knoxville.

The brandy they'd produced was damn good. So for the past two years, Max and his sister, Zora, the company's VP of sales, had been trying to convince their father to move forward with bringing a KFD brandy to market.

His father agreed that the quality was outstanding. Still, he hadn't been ready to commit to expanding the company's basic product line beyond the limited-edition moonshines they'd rolled out in honor of the company's jubilee three years ago.

He would pick the day I feel like I've been run over by a truck to discuss this.

"Print me a copy of everything you have on—"

Molly shoved a binder with colored tabs in his direction. "That's everything. Oh, and I took the liberty of updating the projected sales numbers. I also created a quick summary of the key selling points. It's on page one."

Note to self: get Molly that limited edition Star Wars electric pressure cooker she's been eyeing for her birthday.

She finished briefing him on the materials, then urged him in the direction of the conference room, armed with a fresh cup of coffee, promptly at five minutes to eleven,.

At least now he more closely resembled a fully functioning human being.

Max entered the room and slid into his usual chair beside Zora.

"Glad you could join us," his sister whispered, elbowing him in the ribs. "I thought we might need to send someone to revive you."

"Ha-ha." He didn't look in his sister's direction. Instead, he focused on the older man seated on the other side of the table whose snow-white hair and beard contrasted his dark brown skin. "Good morning, Mr. Bazemore."

"Morning, Max." A wide smile spread across Dixon Bazemore's face as they both rose to their feet and shook hands. The old man had been the owner of Bazemore Orchards longer than Max had been alive. "Good to see you, young man."

"You, too, Mr. B." Molly's instincts about the reason for the meeting had been right. Why else would Dixon Bazemore be here? Still, he asked, "What brings you to see us today?"

"We'll go over everything during the meeting," Max's father interjected. "We're waiting for one more person."

Max glanced around the table. All of the members of the executive committee were present. His grandfather and father. His brothers Blake and Parker, the operations VP and CFO, respectively. Blake's wife, Savannah—the company's events manager. Zora, him and his father's admin, Lianna, who was there to take notes.

"Who are we—"

"I'm sorry. I got a little turned around finding my way back here from the parking lot. But I've got your portfolio, Grandad."

Max snapped his attention in the direction of the familiar voice. He hadn't heard it in more than a decade, but he would never, *ever* forget it. His mouth went dry, and his heart thudded so loudly he was sure his sister could hear it.

"Peaches?" He scanned the brown eyes that stared back at him through narrowed slits.

"Quinn." She was gorgeous, despite the slightly

irritated flare of her nostrils and the stiff smile that barely revealed her dimples. "Hello, Max."

The *good to see you* was notably absent. But what should he expect? It was his fault they hadn't parted on the best of terms.

Quinn settled into the empty seat beside her grandfather. She handed the old man a worn leather portfolio, then squeezed his arm. The genuine smile that lit her brown eyes and activated those killer dimples was firmly in place again.

Max had been the cause of that magnificent smile nearly every day that summer between his junior and senior years of college when he'd interned at Bazemore Orchards.

"Now that everyone is here, we can discuss the matter at hand." His father nodded toward Lianna, and she handed out bound presentations.

"As you can see, we're here to discuss adding fruit brandies to the King's Finest Distillery lineup—a venture Dad, Max and Zora have been pushing for some time." Duke nodded in their general direction. "I think the company and the market are in a good place now for us to explore the possibility."

"Excellent." His sister beamed. "Would this be a permanent addition to the product lineup?"

"I'll only commit to a limited-edition trial." Duke frowned slightly. He always did what was best for their family-owned distillery. But Zora—the youngest and the only girl in a family of four boys—was still his "princess," and his father hated disappointing her. "But if the numbers support it, as with the special-edition moonshines we introduced a few years ago, I'm willing to discuss making the line permanent."

"Bourbon is what we're known for," Parker, also known as Negative Ned, chimed in. "Won't adding other liquors to the lineup dilute our brand?"

Parker wasn't being argumentative. He was painstakingly methodical and questioned everything. It was the way his intricate mind worked.

Zora rolled her eyes and folded her arms, not bothering to hide her annoyance. "Pepsi sells several types of soda, water, tea, juice and energy drinks. It hasn't damaged their reputation as a top beverage company."

Parker thought about Zora's words for a moment, then nodded sagely. He scribbled on the ever-present pad in front of him and pushed his glasses up the bridge of his nose. "Good point. Go on."

Duke fought back a chuckle, then continued.

Max should have been riveted by the conversation. After all, this project was one he'd been fighting for over the past thirty months. Yet, it took every ounce of self-control he could muster to keep from blatantly staring at the beautiful woman seated directly across the table from him.

Peaches. Or rather, Quinn Bazemore. Dixon Bazemore's granddaughter. She was more gorgeous than he remembered. Her beautiful, deep brown skin looked silky and smooth.

The simple gray shift dress she wore did its best to mask her shape. Still, it was obvious her hips and breasts were fuller now than they'd been the last time he'd held her in his arms. The last time he'd seen every square inch of that shimmering brown skin.

Zora elbowed him again and he held back an audible *oomph.*

"What's with you?" she whispered.

"Nothing," he whispered back.

Maybe he wasn't doing such a good job of masking his fascination with Quinn.

Max opened his booklet to the page his father indicated. He was thrilled that the company was ready to give their brandy initiative a try, even if it was just a test run.

He understood why Mr. Bazemore was there. His farm had been providing the fruit for the brandy and would continue to do so. But that didn't explain the presence of his ex.

Quinn shifted in her seat beneath Max Abbott's heated stare. She refused to glance in his direction. She wasn't here to flirt with the handsome-as-ever Max Abbott. She'd come to King's Finest Distillery for two reasons: to help save her grandfather's farm and to build a case study for the consultancy she'd launch as soon as the farm was on stable ground again.

It was a venture she'd mused about as an undergrad. But she'd settled into a comfortable public relations career instead. Until six months ago, when she'd found herself out of a job and unable to work in her field within a fifty-mile radius of her home in Atlanta.

With no immediate plans, she'd packed up her condo and accepted her grandfather's invitation to their family farm just outside of Knoxville, where she'd spent her summers as a kid.

Just until she figured out her next move.

The excitement of helping her grandfather establish important strategic partnerships revived her interest in her forgotten venture. So she'd dusted off her business plan, plugged in the holes and improved on it. Now she needed to build her portfolio while she waited out the remaining six months of the non-compete clause in her employment agreement with her former PR firm. Then she'd return to Atlanta and launch her new practice.

This proposed partnership with the world-renowned King's Finest Distillery would be the cornerstone of her growing portfolio. So if that meant pretending not to be affected by the man who'd broken her heart and crushed it into minuscule pieces without so much as a backward glance, she'd suck it up and do just that.

If Max could behave as if that summer between them had never happened, so could she.

Duke was explaining that they would begin the venture with apple-, peach- and cherry-flavored brandies, and that all of the fruit would be sourced from Bazemore Farms.

Quinn's heart swelled when everyone in the room applauded. She was relieved no one had objected to making her grandfather's farm the sole source for the fruit. It was a sweet deal for the farm, which had been struggling in recent years. Partly because of a shift in the market and how difficult it had become to get solid, reliable help at a price the farm could sustainably afford. Partly because of the shady accountant who'd taken over the books after her grandmother's death several years ago.

"This will be a co-branded product, something we've never done before. A partnership that was brokered by Dixon's lovely granddaughter, Quinn." Duke gestured toward her. "She's here in her capacity as an executive of Bazemore Farms, but she's also a collaboration expert. We had a fine chat last week about some of her innovative ideas for quickly getting this venture to market. Quinn."

"Thank you, Mr. Abbott." Quinn stood, pulling a stack of presentations from her bag. She walked around the table, placing one in front of each person as she explained how she'd created lucrative partnerships between clients in the past.

"As a rep at one of Atlanta's most prestigious PR firms for the past eight years, I…" Quinn stammered, unsettled by the jolt of heat that surged through her when Max's eyes met hers as she handed him a copy of the presentation.

It was her nerves, *not* Max Abbott, that had caused her words to come out in a jumble.

Despite the silent outrage in the widened eyes framed by thick, neat brows, the man was still devastatingly handsome. He was a little older and his shoulders were a bit broader. But he looked essentially like the boy she'd fallen in love with that one passionate summer. The last she'd spent with her grandparents before going off to college. The summer Max had been an intern, living and working on the farm.

That was more than a decade ago. Time had treated him well.

"I've handled sensitive public relations campaigns for some of the biggest names in fintech," she continued.

"We already have a PR person," Parker interrupted, shoving his glasses up the bridge of his nose.

"You have a college student who handles social media, your newsletter, and the occasional press release." Quinn maintained her warm smile. Duke had warned her Parker would be a tough nut to crack, and that Max and Zora might be insulted by the idea of bringing her on to execute the project that had been their baby. "But a project of this magnitude requires a dedicated, experienced professional who'll get vendors and consumers excited about the new product line. Just as Savannah did for the company's jubilee and the associated release of limited-edition moonshines a few years ago."

Savannah smiled approvingly, and Parker nodded in agreement, silenced for the moment.

"If you'll turn to page five, we can quickly review a rundown of how I'm proposing to help King's Finest and Bazemore Farms make the most of this joint venture."

"You're bringing in someone else to execute our proposal?" Max ignored her completely, asking the question of his father instead. "Zora and I are fully capable of—"

"Speak for yourself, big brother." Zora turned her chair toward him before their father could respond. "I have a lot on my plate. We've seen a real uptick in our international sales and domestic market share in regions outside of the South since the jubilee. I'm traveling extensively over the next few months. I can't add another thing to my to-do list right now. Neither can my team. As long as we're consulted regularly, I'm all for bringing someone else on to do the heavy lifting."

Quinn exhaled quietly, and her racing heart slowed in response to Zora's encouraging nod.

"And you've had your hands full with the expansion of our marketing efforts," Duke reminded him.

"So it would be better to have someone wholly dedicated to the project."

Max's nostrils flared, and a streak of red bloomed across his forehead and cheeks. He opened his mouth to object further, but his grandfather cut him off.

"Let Quinn finish her presentation, son. Then we can discuss any concerns privately and make our final decision." Joseph Abbott nodded in her direction. "Please continue, Quinn."

She smiled gratefully at the older man she'd always called Grandpa Joe, then inhaled deeply, smiled broadly and put on the presentation of her life.

She'd won over Joseph and Duke Abbott, the company's founder and CEO. Zora and Savannah were also on board. Blake, she couldn't quite read but Parker and Max definitely required convincing. So that was what she would do.

In this room, in this moment, Max Abbott wasn't her first love, her first real kiss, her first…*everything*. He was a skeptical company executive, not unlike the dozens she'd encountered before in her career.

Despite whatever else Max might be feeling toward her—curiosity, animosity, maybe even attraction—he was a sensible individual. And like every other Abbott at the table, she knew he wanted what was best for King's Finest.

She just needed to convince him that she was the best person for the job. And convince herself that working with her ex wasn't her worst idea ever. Her entire future was riding on it.

Two

Max groaned quietly as Quinn finished her presentation. He'd sifted through her proposal and listened carefully, ready to poke holes in it and rip it apart. But the plan was solid, and Quinn had suggested useful partnerships he and Zora hadn't considered.

Still, this project was *his* and Zora's baby. They'd taken their grandfather's request to add flavored brandies to the lineup seriously. Had worked with him to develop it. Worn their father down until he'd agreed to invest in the stills and bring in an expert brandy distiller. Revisited the topic at *every* damn quarterly meeting for the past two years. So for his father to just hand off the project to his ex of all the goddamned people on the face of God's green earth… Yeah, it felt a hell of a lot like a solid knee in the nuts. Even if no one in the room besides him and Quinn were aware of their romantic history.

But his father was right. He and Zora had their hands full with all of the additional business King's Finest was doing. Much of it could be credited to the efforts of his sister-in-law, Savannah, who'd become their de facto PR person since she'd joined the company three years ago. Savannah handled event management for both the distillery and the renovated barn on the edge of his parents' property, which they rented out for weddings and other events.

The company's event and tour business was booming now. But Savannah was six months pregnant with her and Blake's second child, and their two-year-old son was already a handful. The last thing his sister-in-law needed was another project.

"Well, what do you think?" Grandpa Joseph beamed. Dixon and Quinn had been dispatched on an hour-long tour of the King's Finest Distillery while the Abbotts formally debated the Bazemore Farms proposal. "That one's a sharp cookie, eh?" His grandfather chuckled. "I remember the first time I met Quinn. She was about three years old and she had more questions than any kid that age I'd ever encountered besides Zora." He grinned at his only granddaughter.

"I love the plan she put together for us." Zora thumbed through the document Quinn had prepared. "Having her handle all of this is a godsend. And she's got the right personality for the job. She didn't skip a beat or get frustrated with Parker's myriad questions or Max's pushback." Zora raised an eyebrow at him. "And I love her suggestions for finding new ways to partner with state and local vendors."

"Excellent. Blake, how about you?" Duke asked Max's eldest brother, the heir apparent to the King's Finest CEO–ship.

"I love everything about the plan." Blake tapped the cover of the presentation. "I like Quinn, and I know the distributors will like her, too. If she can do half of what she's presented here, I'm sold."

"Parker?" Duke turned to him, as if prepared for the worst.

Parker scanned the data again. "The numbers look good. If you're sure we can do this without compromising our position in the bourbon market…" He shrugged. "I'm fine with moving forward on a trial basis. Say…six months once it goes to market. If sales are good, we can talk long-term."

"Sounds fair." Duke nodded, then turned to him. "And what say you, Max?"

Max released a quiet breath. Every eye in the room was focused on him. Quinn's plan was flawless; he had no legitimate reason to object to it.

So what was he going to say?

That he didn't want to work with her because it would be a constant reminder that he'd been a complete dick to her thirteen years ago?

"The plan is fine…okay, it's good," he amended in response to everyone's guffaws and raised eyebrows. "It's damn good. I'll give you that. But this is *our* company." He tapped the table with his index finger. "*Our* project. A project we're doing in memory of Savannah's grandfather Martin. Don't you think *we* should be the ones to handle it rather than bringing in an outsider?"

Had that come off as spoiled and elitist as it sounded in his head?

God, I hope not.

"Seriously, dude? *She's not one of us,*" Zora mimicked him in a whiny, low voice. "*That's* the best you can do?"

Everyone at the table laughed.

"You gotta admit, that argument is weak sauce, bruh." Blake chuckled. "Quinn is an experienced professional and she and Mr. B are good people."

"And I know she's not technically family, but I wouldn't exactly call her an *outsider,* either," Grandpa Joe added, sounding a little hurt by the dig. "I've always been quite fond of the girl. Considered her an honorary granddaughter."

"I know, Gramps. And I didn't mean anything by it." Max sighed and scrubbed a hand down his face. "I guess what I'm saying is that I have a lot of time and energy invested in this project. So the idea of relinquishing complete control of it isn't sitting well with me."

"I can respect that, Max." His father nodded sagely as he rubbed his whiskered chin. He leaned forward on one elbow. "What can we do to make you more comfortable with Quinn running point on the project?"

Translation: This is *happening, son. You've been outvoted.*

"I want to be the point person on this project internally," Max said definitively. "And it should be clear that Quinn reports to me."

"Done." His father shrugged. "That'll leave me more time to golf. Anything else?"

"I plan to be as involved in the project as my schedule permits." Max folded his hands on the table in front of him. "And I need to have the option to terminate the agreement early should I find just cause."

Duke stroked his chin as he silently contemplated Max's request. He nodded begrudgingly. "Agreed, but I get the final say on such a drastic action."

"Perfect." Grandpa Joe slapped the table and chuckled. "Lianna, order us some lunch. We've got reason to celebrate. And make sure to break out the good mason jars so we can all sample a little of that brandy."

Just peachy.

He'd be working closely with the one ex who had it out for him. The stiff smile she'd given him when he'd used her nickname made it obvious she was still harboring a grudge that would impede their working relationship. This project was too important to his grandfather and their company. He wouldn't permit his past mistake to interfere with family business. He'd handle this the way he handled every other business problem: by facing it head-on.

That meant clearing the air with Quinn the first opportunity he got.

The Bazemores had returned to the conference room where a selection of pastas from a local Italian restaurant awaited them. They'd shared a meal with the Abbotts and sampled the peach, apple and cherry brandies. All of them were remarkably good.

Max's father and grandfather had invited Dixon to join them for a celebratory round of golf and, doubtless, more drinking. Parker had left to walk Cricket—his fiancée Kayleigh Jemison's golden retriever. That left Zora, Quinn, Blake and Savannah, who were seated at the table chatting after the meal.

Quinn was mooning over the adorable photos of Max's nephew, Davis, on Blake's phone.

Max had waited patiently, not actively joining in the conversation, instead staying engaged and nodding or chuckling whenever warranted. He needed a moment alone with Quinn.

He glanced at the text message that flashed on his watch: The league wants to talk sponsorship in an hour. We need to review notes.

For the past several months he'd been working on a sponsorship deal with the Memphis Marauders professional football team. Turning down the call wasn't an option. But he didn't want to put off clearing the air with Quinn, either.

If they were going to work together, they needed to start off with a clean slate.

Max stood abruptly and everyone in the room turned toward him. He cleared his throat. "Hey guys, I need to speak with Quinn for a moment...*privately*," he added, for the benefit of his sister, who'd shrugged.

Blake and Savannah exchanged a puzzled look.

"Yeah, sure." Blake stood, helping his wife up.

Savannah rubbed her growing belly. "It was a pleasure to meet you, Quinn. Lianna will give you my contact information. I'd love to meet for lunch later this week."

Blake and Savannah left, hand in hand. Zora folded her arms.

"Zora." Max gave her his *I'm not bullshitting right now* voice. A voice he'd had to employ often over the years with his little sister.

"Fine." Zora stood, then looked at Quinn. "As long as you're okay with this."

"It's fine, but thank you, Zora." Quinn smiled politely as she stood, gathering her papers. A clear sign that she was leaving, too.

Zora shot Max a warning look and breezed out of the room.

As soon as the door closed behind his sister, Quinn turned to him and scowled. "Why would you give everyone the impression something is going on between us?"

He tried not to take her words personally, but damn if it didn't feel like she'd kicked him in the teeth wearing a pair of steel toe boots.

There was a time when her greatest desire had been for them to go out on a proper date and let the world see them together. Rather than sneaking around and hooking up in his shabby little loft over the barn or in the bed of his truck, parked beneath the stars.

Heat stung his cheeks as he jammed his hands into his pockets. "They probably assume I want to talk about the project or catch up with an old friend."

He pretended not to notice the way she pressed her lips together and furrowed her brows when he referred to them as *friends*.

Damn. Is there a draft in here?

The chilly vibe coming from his ex was all too real.

"And I really would love to catch up at some point. But first, I need to tell you just how sorry I am."

"No." She shook her head, her tousled beach waves swinging gently.

He curled the fingers still shoved into his pockets into tight fists. Max couldn't help remembering how he'd sifted the soft strands through his fingers as she had lain in his arms. And the dreamy way she'd gazed up at him after they'd made love.

There was nothing remotely romantic about the frosty look Quinn cast in his direction from beneath her long, thick eyelashes.

"No, you won't allow me to apologize to you, or no, you're not willing to accept my sincere apology?" He sat on the edge of the conference table.

"Both." Quinn folded her arms, her expression neutral. Despite the iciness that slid over his skin in response to her answer, her tone and expression betrayed no anger. "A—I don't want your apology. B—There's no need for it."

Heat spanned his forehead. Max had imagined having this conversation with Quinn dozens of times. He'd envisioned anger, forgiveness and lots of incredibly hot makeup sex. What he hadn't foreseen was Quinn standing here calm, callous and completely out of fucks to give.

Not that he didn't deserve it.

"I appreciate you saying that, Quinn. But I'd feel better if—"

"No." Her voice vibrated with thinly veiled anger this time and her eyes narrowed. "You don't get to do this."

"I don't get to do what? Apologize?" Max was genuinely stunned by her refusal.

"You don't get to absolve yourself of guilt this way." Quinn raked her fingers through her hair and tucked a few strands behind her ear. "It's been thirteen years. If you didn't see fit to apologize before now, I can't imagine that your apology is sincere. So let's not do this, *please*."

The soft, pleading tone with which she ended her request reminded him of how she'd uttered his name during those sultry summer nights.

Max winced and swallowed hard. His hushed tone matched hers. "You have every right to be angry with me, Quinn."

"I wasn't angry, Max. I was hurt." Her stony expression faltered momentarily. "By the end of that summer you'd proclaimed your undying love for me. Then as soon as you returned to campus you broke up with me via a one-sided, two-minute phone call. For months, I wondered what I'd done wrong. I finally realized that it wasn't anything I'd done." She shrugged, her smile returning. "You were just an ass. A handsome, charming one. But an ass nevertheless."

"On that we can agree." He sighed, folding his arms.

She flashed the triumphant half smile he remembered so well.

"If there's nothing else, I should go." She lifted her bag onto her shoulder. "We can meet in the morning to strategize, if that works for you."

"Are you staying at the farm?" he asked.

"I am," she said in a tone that made it clear she felt the question too personal. "Why?"

"You have nearly an hour drive to get here." He walked her toward the door. "So you name the time."

"Ten o'clock?"

"See you then." His heart thudded as he watched her slip out the door.

He'd screwed up by walking away from Quinn the

way he had. Now those chickens had come home to roost.

Max groaned quietly as he sank onto a nearby chair. He and Quinn would only need to work closely together at the outset of the project. After that, they could work together remotely, when necessary. He could certainly keep it together for a few months.

Shit.

It was the same lie he'd told himself when he'd first laid eyes on Quinn that summer.

Just look at how that turned out.

Three

Quinn changed her outfit for the third time this morning. It was unlike her. She was organized and decisive. With her planner on hand, she was always ready for the day ahead. But she hadn't slept well last night. It didn't help that she'd drifted off while reviewing her notes for her upcoming meeting with Max.

He'd seemed disappointed to discover that her proposal was a good one. He'd clearly been expecting her to flop. And if she did, Max would no doubt be ready to pull the plug on their project. So there was no room for failure, fear or hesitance. She had to show up today at Max's office with her game face on. Make it clear that she knew *exactly* what she was doing.

This deal meant too much to her grandfather's farm and to her future. So she wouldn't allow herself to be intimidated by the fact that Max clearly didn't want her there. Nor would she be distracted by Max's good looks, his charm or the fact that when his eyes met hers she still felt...*something* for him.

When she'd seen him yesterday, a jolt of electricity had rocketed up her spine. His dark eyes had seemed to peer straight through her, like armor-piercing rounds shredding her flesh, despite the mental suit of armor she'd donned before she'd stepped into the room.

The truth was that she hadn't gotten lost on her way back to the conference room that morning. She'd simply needed a moment to compose herself before she came face-to-face with Max again.

It'd been thirteen years since she'd seen Max Abbott, more than a third of her thirty-one years. Enough time to give her distance and perspective. Enough time to realize that Max Abbott hadn't been as important in the overall scheme of her life as her teenage brain had once believed.

Yes, he'd been her first love, and over that long, hot summer she'd allowed herself to believe that Max was the alpha and omega of her romantic life. That there would never be another man for her.

Quinn laughed bitterly. *God, you were naive.*

Unfortunately, she hadn't learned her lesson after Max. She'd still wanted to believe that people were inherently good and could be taken at their word. Her most recent ex had finally cured her of her Pollyanna-ish misconceptions.

The cold, hard fact was that there were a lot more liars in the world than there were people she could count on. But her grandfather was firmly in the latter camp. She wouldn't disappoint him by allowing her inconvenient history with Max to sabotage this deal.

Quinn followed the smell of pancakes, bacon and coffee down the stairs. Her grandfather stood over the sizzling cast-iron pan with a spatula in hand.

The memory of her grandmother—vibrant and beautiful until the day she died—standing there in the kitchen, cooking in that pan, with that spatula, flashed through Quinn's brain. Her mouth curved in a faint smile, though her chest suddenly felt heavy.

"You've got her smile, you know." Her grandfather's voice startled her from the daze she'd fallen into.

"I know." Quinn's smile deepened. She set the heels she was wearing today by the kitchen door. "And I love that I'll always have that connection to her."

She didn't bother to ask how her grandfather knew she'd been thinking of her grandmother. It was hard not to enter what had been Lydia Bazemore's domain and *not* think of her.

"Maybe you'll have a little girl someday with that same smile." Her grandfather winked, chuckling when she rolled her eyes and groaned in response. "Hey, an old man can dream."

"Hate to break it to you, Gramps, but there are zero prospects of a great-granddaughter on the horizon. At least not from me." She kissed her grandfather on his stubbly cheek. "I can't speak for Marcus and Mavis," she said of her younger twin siblings.

"I don't think the world is ready for the progeny of Marcus or Mavis." Her grandfather laughed, and she did, too.

Her younger brother and sister were hyperfocused science geeks who lived in their own little world. A world she never quite fit into. They were just five years younger than she was, but with the emotional distance between her and her younger siblings, it might as well have been five light-years.

The two of them were more like their parents— both scientists working in academia—than Quinn would ever be. At the dinner table with her family, she'd always felt like the answer to one of those *Sesame Street* skits: *Which one of these doesn't belong?*

"One day." He smiled. "Just not today." Her grandfather nodded toward the coffeemaker. "Grab yourself a cup of coffee and have a seat. I know you have to get out of here soon."

Quinn didn't argue. Instead, she poured herself a cup of coffee and added creamer from the fridge. Then she pulled out one of the yellow-vinyl-and-chrome chairs from beneath the chrome and yellow Formica table. Her grandparents had owned the vintage set for years, and, despite its age, it was in excellent shape. She sank onto the chair.

Her grandparents had always been frugal and sensible, saving up for when they'd leave the farm to their children or grandchildren and then travel the world. But none of their children or grandchildren had ever taken an interest in owning the farm. And then her grandmother had died suddenly of a stroke a few years ago, leaving her grandfather devastated.

Since Quinn had come to stay with him a few months ago, he'd been the happiest she'd seen him since the death of her grandmother. Maybe it was because her smile reminded him of his beloved wife's. Or maybe it was because it had given him a new purpose—fussing over her.

Her grandfather brought their plates to the table and they settled into their usual morning rhythm. Only there was nothing usual about this morning. Today she would return to King's Finest, where she and Max would start working together on this project.

"You must've had a good time at the country club yesterday." Quinn put a forkful of the buttery pancakes in her mouth and chewed.

"We did." He nodded. "And I would've told you all about it, but you were knocked out when I got back. I put all of your paperwork on your desk and draped one of your grandmother's quilts over you." He sipped some of his coffee. "You haven't crashed like that since the day you first arrived here from Atlanta. When you were so stressed-out it was like you were all tied in knots."

There was an odd stretch of silence between them as he nibbled on his bacon and she ate her pancakes.

"You seemed tense in the meeting yesterday." He peered at her over his coffee cup. "Particularly with Max." He set his cup down and folded his arms on the table, his dark eyes assessing hers. "Everything okay between you two?"

"Of course." Quinn drank long and deep from her coffee mug before lowering it. She forced a smile much bigger and brighter than the occasion called for. "Why wouldn't it be? I haven't seen him since I was eighteen."

One of her grandfather's wiry eyebrows seemed to levitate. He frowned. "You remember *exactly* how long it's been since you've seen the boy?"

Quinn froze, her smile still in place.

"It was the summer before I went to college." She stuffed more pancakes in her mouth and chewed.

"But there's no bad blood between you two, right? I mean, you got on well enough the summer he interned for me, but if there's something I need to know—"

"There isn't." Quinn placed a hand on her grandfather's forearm. Her voice was firm as she met his gaze. "Everything is fine."

"You're sure? Because I sensed some tension on his side of the table, too. When you walked in that door, it was like the boy had seen a ghost."

It'd felt that way for her, too, though she'd had the advantage of expecting that ghost and bracing for it.

"Well, like I said, we haven't seen each other in… what…?" She made a show of counting in her head. "Thirteen years. That's bound to surprise someone, right?" She laughed nervously. "As for the tension… Look at it from Max's perspective. He's the VP of marketing and I come waltzing in the door with my fancy plan. To him, it must feel like a challenge to his authority. Like I'm saying I can do his job better than he can. But it's not about that. It's about this single joint project and how we can make it amazing by thinking more broadly about opportunities for collaboration."

Her grandfather nodded and sighed—a sure sign he wasn't convinced of her explanation for the tension he'd noticed.

"Well, you don't want to be late on your first day." He stood, collecting his dishes. "Leave everything when you're done. I'll clear the table."

Quinn ate the last of her bacon and finished her coffee. "Thanks, Gramps." She got up, pushed her chair under the table and kissed his cheek again. "I'll keep you posted on how things go today. But don't wait up for me. By the time I drive back from Magnolia Lake, it'll probably be pretty late."

He stopped running the water in the sink and frowned. "You know I believe in doing things face-to-face rather than on the phone or those video calls. But I hate that you'll be on the road so much."

"I know, but it won't be forever. Just until we get everything sorted out and in motion."

"Still, it's an hour each way. Maybe we should rent a place for you in Magnolia Lake for a few months."

"Things are already tight around here." Quinn hated bringing it up. Her grandfather felt bad enough about being so distraught over the death of his wife that he hadn't noticed the accountant he'd hired to manage the books—something her grandmother had handled—was robbing him blind.

It had been Quinn's distinct pleasure to throw the guy out on his ass and report him to the local sheriff.

"I know." He nodded solemnly. "But I'd never forgive myself if something happened to you. So keep an eye out for a room or apartment you can rent short term. I'll ask around at the senior center—"

"Not necessary." Quinn shook her head vehemently. She'd end up staying in some creepy room filled with dolls or cats or hooked up on a blind date with someone's worthless grandson.

No thanks.

"I'll handle it. You just worry about sticking it to them in the next Scrabble tournament." Quinn grinned at her grandfather.

Her grandfather raised his fists and shuffled his feet

as he bobbed and weaved, doing his best Muhammad Ali imitation. "This time, I'm gonna take every last one of those suckers out."

Quinn laughed. Her grandfather was still smarting over his second-place finish in the last tournament. "I know you will, Grandad."

She got into the Honda her younger brother had gifted her when the lease for her expensive import had ended. Here in rural Tennessee, she couldn't get anywhere without a reliable car, and she'd never learned to drive her grandfather's truck—a stick shift.

It was a long drive, and she used the time to review the plan in her head while listening to something soothing and upbeat.

Prepare the plan. Don't worry about the man.

That would be her motto as long as she worked with Max. Still, she couldn't help thinking about how handsome he looked. Or how incredible he smelled. The heat she'd felt standing so close to him when the two of them were alone. His pained expression when she wouldn't accept his apology.

She shut her eyes and sighed. It didn't matter if she was still attracted to him. It didn't matter that her memories of that summer had come roaring back to her in her sleep, as vivid as the day they'd occurred. Her summer fling with Max was a part of her distant past. And that was exactly where it would stay.

Four

Max glided into the office well ahead of his usual start time, but not early enough to beat his assistant.

"Mmm…doughnuts." Molly's eyes danced with excitement when she caught a glimpse of the small box in his hand. "Did you get—"

"A bear claw for you?" He grinned, holding up a separate bag in the same hand as his cup of coffee. "Of course."

She thanked him, accepting the bag. Molly tilted her head as she scanned him for a moment.

"What is it?" He looked down at his shirt. Had he spilled coffee on it?

"You look…nice," she said. Only Molly Halloran could pay someone a compliment and still make it sound like an accusation.

"That's a good thing, right?" He unlocked his

office door. "Besides, I'd like to think I look nice every day."

"You do." She trailed him into the office. "But today it feels like you *tried* to look good, and you went a little heavy on the cologne. So I'm guessing this is for the benefit of Ms. Bazemore." Molly stated the facts as if they were the elements of a math equation. Two plus two equals four. She studied his expression, then nodded. "You're definitely into her."

Max wouldn't debate Molly's conclusion, and neither was there reason for him to give it credence. "Remember what we talked about, Mol. Use your deductive powers for good. Not to analyze my romantic interests."

"Right," Molly took a bite of her bear claw as she contemplated his words. "The doughnuts were a nice gesture, since you obviously aren't happy about having to work with her on this project." She put the rest of the bear claw back in the bag and closed it. "I'm going to get one of those cake stands of your mother's from the break room. It'll make a nice display."

"Sounds great. Thanks." He settled behind his desk and took a deep breath, glad for a few minutes alone with his thoughts.

It'd been nearly twenty-four hours since he'd seen Quinn Bazemore again, and his head was still swimming. The memories of their summer fling had kept him up all night, tossing and turning.

He hadn't thought about Quinn in so long. And now he couldn't think about anything else. There had been something so authentically joyful about her. He couldn't ever recall laughing and grinning more than he had during those few months.

Max remembered the first time he'd laid eyes on her that summer. He hadn't seen Quinn since she'd been ten and he'd been thirteen. He'd been stunned that the annoying little chatterbox in pigtails had grown up to be the sexy, long-legged temptress in front of him. And yet, he'd feigned a complete lack of interest and maintained his distance.

Their grandfathers were close friends. Getting involved with her could only mean trouble.

But she'd been flirtatious, persistent, funny and just so damn... Quinn. She'd cut through his resolve to ignore her like a hot knife slicing through whipped butter.

How could he *not* have fallen for her?

Quinn had been gorgeous with her dark brown skin and her thick, black hair pulled back in a single braid. She was bright and amusing. Thoughtful and opinionated. Hopeful yet pragmatic. She'd stimulated his curiosity about the world beyond his privileged purview more than anyone or anything else had. He'd loved seeing the world through her eyes and debating all manner of issues with her.

And there was something mesmerizing about her brown eyes. He still remembered the first time she'd gazed at him like he was everything she'd ever wanted. It was one of those nights she'd snuck up to his loft with leftovers in tow and they'd played video games while debating which male tennis player would win the US Open that year.

She'd been right, as she so often was.

Max sighed softly. He'd felt incredibly lucky to be the object of Quinn's admiring gaze. He'd also felt unworthy of it. But when she'd leaned in and pressed her mouth to his, he'd been an absolute goner. One kiss was all it had taken to get him completely addicted to the sweet taste of her mouth. To the lush feel of her soft curves pressed against him.

The look Quinn had given him when he'd called her *Peaches* at yesterday's meeting was the complete opposite of how she'd regarded him when he used the affectionate moniker back then. Max knifed his fingers through his headful of short curls and groaned quietly. He would never forget the fleeting look of abject disgust in the same brown eyes that had once shone with deep affection.

A knock at the door startled Max.

"Quinn." He stood suddenly, tipping over his cup of coffee. The dark brown liquid spread, soaking the papers on his desk, including the presentation he'd been reviewing.

Not a good look, man.

"Sorry, I didn't mean to startle you." Quinn dropped her bags near the door and quickly scanned the room. She spotted a stack of napkins on the small table in the corner of his office. Quinn grabbed a handful and blotted the mess while he stood there, frozen, staring at her. "I realize I'm a few minutes early, but your assistant was away from her desk, so I just knocked. I didn't mean to—"

"You're fine," he said. He swallowed hard, his cheeks heating as his rogue eyes quickly scanned her deliciously curvy form, highlighted by the fitted skirt and blouse she wore. "I mean...*it's* fine." He finally sprang into action, grabbing a handful of napkins and dabbing at the wet papers. "I shouldn't have been sitting here daydreaming."

"Garbage can?" Quinn asked.

He grabbed the trashcan from beneath his desk and held it up so she could drop the wet napkins into it. "I've got this."

"I don't mind." Her gaze met his momentarily. "After all, I feel partly responsible."

"You shouldn't," he said. *Really.*

Molly rushed into the room with the sparkling-clean glass-domed cake stand.

"Sorry it took me so long, but I had to wash this. It's been sitting on top of the refrigerator for a few months and—" She stopped short when she noticed Max wasn't alone. "Oh, you must be Ms. Bazemore."

"It's Quinn." She moved toward Molly with her hand extended and a warm smile on her face.

She's even more beautiful than she was that summer. How is that even fucking possible?

"It's a pleasure to meet you…"

"Molly. Molly Halloran." His assistant shook Quinn's hand. "It's a pleasure to meet you, too."

"I'm afraid that I'm to blame for this mess. I startled Max when I came in just now," Quinn said. "Would you have something I can clean it up with? Disinfectant wipes, maybe?"

"No worries. I'll take care of it, Ms.…Quinn." Molly shifted her gaze to Max and gave him a *what happened?* look. "Can I get you some coffee or maybe a doughnut?" Molly set the cake stand on the small table in the corner and then used the wax paper to carefully arrange each doughnut on the glass stand.

"Is that raspberry jelly–filled?" Quinn pointed to one of the doughnuts.

"It is." Max remembered how much she'd loved them.

Quinn momentarily glanced up from beneath her thick lashes before returning her attention to the assortment. She picked up the raspberry jelly–filled doughnut and took a bite.

"It's delicious. Thank you," she muttered through a mouthful. "That was thoughtful of you."

He exhaled quietly and shoved a hand in his pocket. It was his peace offering since she wouldn't allow him to apologize for how he'd ended things between them.

Molly quickly cleaned up the mess, promised to reprint the ruined documents and left the room.

"Have a seat, please." Max pulled out the closest chair for Quinn, then took his own across from her.

She put down her partially eaten doughnut and wiped the powdered sugar from her hands and mouth with a napkin. She reached into her bag and pulled out two binders: one thick, one thin.

"I thought we could start by going through the plan I laid out yesterday. You can tell me what works for you and if there's anything you object to. Then we can establish an agenda for the next six months."

Six months. He gritted his teeth.

Max had managed to get through more than a decade without running into Quinn even once, despite the friendship that their grandfathers shared. And now he was being forced to work with her for half a year.

Peachy.

"Excellent idea," he said. "Because I'd like to make a few amendments."

He didn't intend to insult her; this was business, not personal. His first obligation was to his family and King's Finest. If Quinn couldn't handle that, he needed to know now.

"Amendments?" Quinn frowned. "Like what?"

Molly brought Max a fresh cup of coffee and the newly printed copies. She was gone as quickly as she'd entered the room.

"You were saying?" Quinn's posture was stiff.

"You've suggested that we have representation at numerous domestic and international distributor conventions."

"Yes?"

"It's a great idea, in theory," he said. "In reality, the plan feels too ambitious. It represents quite an investment of resources for a six-month trial period. And it would spread me and Zora too thin. We already have a lot on our plates."

"Fair point on the budgetary considerations." She opened her planner and made a few notes. "I know you and Zora are busy. That's why I'm here. I didn't expect either of you to attend the listed events."

"Then who would represent…wait… *You'd* be the lone representative of King's Finest at all of these events?" He pressed his back against the chair. "This distillery is my family's legacy. We don't just sell spirits, Quinn. We sell the storied history of this place… of this family. And, no offense, but yesterday was the first day you've ever set foot in this building. I'm not comfortable sending someone who isn't an Abbott out to represent our family and my grandfather's legacy."

"Grandpa Joe didn't seem to have a problem with it." She folded her arms over her ample chest and his heart beat faster in response.

He dragged his eyes back up to meet hers. "I doubt

he realized that you intended to fly all over the world as the sole representative of our family." He folded his arms, too.

"I discussed this very idea with him." Quinn pursed her lips as she put her elbows on the little table—narrowly avoiding squishing her doughnut. "He didn't express any doubts. After all, I'm an experienced public relations professional, and I've represented billion-dollar organizations."

"I don't doubt your abilities, Quinn. But this isn't an impersonal corporation. Here, everything we do, we take it extremely personally." He tapped his index finger on the table. "Because the King's Finest name is on every single bottle we sell. We're all keenly aware that with each transaction, the crack of every single seal, our family's name and reputation is on the line."

"I can appreciate why this is such a sensitive subject for you." Quinn seemed to make a pained effort to keep her voice even and her expression calm. "However, you seem to forget that my family's name will be on those brandy bottles, too. I have just as much invested in the success of this project as you do. Perhaps more. Because if this venture doesn't deliver results, King's Finest will scrap it and move on. My grandfather might never get another high-visibility opportunity like this again."

"Your job is to protect your grandfather's interest. I respect that. But I need someone on hand whose first interest is this distillery."

Her frown deepened. "You don't believe I'm capable of being equally invested in both our interests?"

"I wouldn't know, Quinn." He shrugged. "We knew each other for one summer thirteen years ago."

"And whose fault is that?" she snapped, then shook her head and inhaled deeply. "No, we're not doing this. We agreed not to revisit the past."

"We didn't *agree*, Quinn. You insisted on it." He pointed out, leaning forward with his arms on the table. "But we need to talk about what happened back then."

"Why? It has no bearing on this project."

"Doesn't it?" He searched her face. "We're less than an hour in and it's already become an issue. Yet, you won't allow me to apologize for my behavior back then."

"Because it isn't—"

"I remember every single word you said yesterday, Quinn, believe me." He held up one hand. "I strongly disagree."

"Is discussing our past a prerequisite for the deal?" she asked.

"Of course not."

"Then I respectfully decline." She looked away, her voice faint. "Sorry I snapped at you—it was a gut reaction, and I apologize." Quinn shifted her gaze back to his. "It's out of my system now. *Really*."

Was he supposed to believe that all of the pent-up anger she'd apparently been harboring had evaporated in an instant? Did she honestly believe that herself?

"That wasn't fair of me." Quinn stood, leaning against the wall behind her. "But you're not being fair, either."

He cocked a brow. "How so?"

"You're arbitrarily rejecting the key component of my plan. And before you claim that you aren't—" she raised a hand to halt his objections "—we both know that you were the only one in that room yesterday who didn't want me working on this project."

She huffed, taking her seat again. "I realize it must be…disappointing to have an outsider work on your pet project. But Max, I'm *really* good at what I do. I'm not asking you to take my word for it. I'm just asking for a fair shot to prove I can deliver everything I promised."

"I know you probably think I'm being an ass just for the hell of it." Something in his chest tightened. "I'm not, Quinn. My fiduciary responsibilities to King's Finest come before any personal relationship—"

"You think I'm asking you to do me a favor because we spent one summer together over a decade ago?" She laughed bitterly.

"Aren't you?" He didn't see what was so funny.

"You expect favors of friends," she said. "We aren't…that. And if you'd consider the plan objectively, you'd see the benefits for King's Finest." She tipped her chin defiantly, her eyes meeting his. "I'm not asking for a personal favor here. I'm asking you to do what's in the best interest of King's Finest, *despite* whatever personal feelings you might have about me."

He hated that she believed he harbored ill feelings toward her. Nothing could be further from the truth. True, he hadn't been eager to work with her. But that was because he hadn't wanted a daily reminder of his blunders where Quinn was concerned, not because he had ill will toward her.

He'd be happy to tell her that if she wasn't so insistent on not discussing their past.

Besides, he would've objected to allowing *anyone*

outside of their family represent the company's interests. Especially someone he hadn't worked with before.

And if there was any resistance to Quinn specifically, it wasn't because he resented her. It was because he wouldn't blame her for resenting him, and he couldn't allow his past blunder to jeopardize King's Finest. Giving Quinn the power to impact the distillery's reputation left him feeling more vulnerable than he was comfortable with.

Max picked up the document and reviewed all the trade shows that Quinn had suggested the company attend. He took his pen and circled five of the domestic listings. "I'm already attending these." He circled three international events. "Zora is attending these." Max put a question mark by two others. "I'll consider these, based on the results of the first three conferences." Finally, he struck a line through the remaining events. "These are off the table for now." He put his pen down and sat back in the chair. "How's that for compromise?"

"Sounds fair." She took the list and read it over. "But where does that leave me? Your father appointed me to take the lead on the project. How can I do that if I'm not attending any of these?"

Max groaned quietly, already regretting what he was about to suggest. "You can accompany me to the first event."

"So... I get to do what? Play Vanna White? Maybe hold up a bottle of brandy while wearing a sparkly dress?" Quinn folded her arms, her leg bouncing.

Was it crazy that he could see that in his head?

"No, of course not." He cleared his throat. "You'd be there to observe and learn."

"Max, I'm not your summer intern. I'm a public relations *expert*," Quinn reminded him. "I don't claim to know everything, but please don't treat me like some clueless novice."

He sighed. "I need to ensure that these trips will provide an acceptable return on investment and that you can handle representing the distillery."

"Then give me a fair shot at demonstrating that." She leaned forward. "You're making your decision based on the first three domestic conferences. So I should attend all three of them."

Quinn stared at him, as if daring him to reject her reasonable suggestion.

He nodded begrudgingly, extending one hand across the table. "Deal."

Max tried to ignore the electricity that tickled his palm when Quinn placed her much smaller hand in his and shook it. The first time he'd held her hand that summer flashed through his brain.

Quinn yanked her hand from his and stood abruptly. "Thank you for giving the plan an honest chance. And for the doughnut. I won't take up any more of your time this morning. I'll get started on some ideas for marketing collateral. I'll need samples of your past marketing campaigns to ensure the look and message are consistent."

"My team will make sure it is." He stood, too. "Molly will get you anything you need. The first event is in a few weeks. Do you think we can turn everything around by then?"

"Absolutely." Quinn didn't hesitate for a moment.

He admired her confidence. She glanced at the small antique watch on her wrist. "I'm meeting with Zora later today, and having lunch with Savannah. They'll help bring me up to speed. And I learned quite a bit on the distillery tour we took while you decided our fate yesterday." She flashed a teasing smile.

"I'll need to review whatever you come up with, and we can bring more of the marketing team in on this to ensure everything is done right and on time," he said as she gathered her things.

"Of course. I'm your partner in this project, Max— not your enemy or rival," she assured him.

"My dad brought you in to head up a project I've been working on for nearly *three years*, Quinn. Maybe it doesn't feel like a competition to you, but it sure as hell feels that way to me," he said gruffly, then quickly changed the topic. "Molly will book your travel, so be sure to give her the necessary info."

"I will. Thank you." Quinn lifted her bag onto her shoulder and raked her fingers through her hair, tugging it over one shoulder.

Max froze for a moment, his eyes drawn to the elegant column of her neck. He'd once trailed kisses down the delicate skin there. Traced a path there with his tongue. He swallowed hard. His pulse quickened, and his throat was suddenly dry.

"I'll have something for you to review by Friday," Quinn said, snapping him out of his brief daze.

"Great. Let's meet first thing Friday morning." His parents' fortieth anniversary party was on Saturday. Savannah was in charge of the arrangements. Still, he expected to get roped into last-minute preparations.

"Oh, and Molly will show you the temporary work-space that's been set up for you."

Quinn thanked him, then left to meet with Molly.

Max returned to his desk to work on the football sponsorship deal still in negotiation. But no matter how much he tried to erase all thoughts of Quinn, the vision of her in that fitted skirt and top just wouldn't leave his brain.

Quinn had obviously written off their past as if it had never happened. Why couldn't he do the same?

Five

Quinn gave Molly the information she needed to make her travel arrangements, then settled into her temporary workspace. She appreciated having her own dedicated space to work. Unfortunately, it provided a direct line of sight to Max's office.

She groaned quietly, then made her way toward the executive floor bathrooms. Standing in front of the mirror, she pressed her hands on the cool granite counter and sucked in a deep breath, her eyes drifting closed momentarily.

Quinn should be proud of herself. She'd shown no visible reaction when her hand had touched Max's—despite the bubbling brew of emotions that had come flooding back to her. She'd forgotten how much larger his hands were than hers. And she'd been drawn in by his enticing masculine scent.

After all this time, just being near Max still made her belly flutter and her temperature rise. Had he noticed the beading of her nipples or how her breath caught? The way her hand trembled in his?

How could something as innocent as a handshake evoke such vivid images and visceral sensations?

Quinn couldn't help thinking of the little touches and stolen kisses they had sneaked in whenever they could on the farm.

The secrecy had made the relationship exciting. It was something for just the two of them. And yet, she'd been bursting to tell someone how giddy and wonderful she felt. Like she was floating in a bubble of contentment. She'd fallen for Max. Hard. And she hadn't been able to imagine going back to a life without him.

Quinn opened her eyes slowly and sifted her fingers through her hair. What she'd felt for Max had been a stupid teenage fantasy. She'd believed him when he professed to love her. When he said he couldn't imagine his life without her, either.

Despite how things had turned out, she couldn't regret being with Max. She regretted her naivete in assigning that chapter in their lives more meaning than it held for him.

Quinn had been the one to pursue Max. She'd barreled right through Max's initial warning that he wasn't looking for a relationship, determined to change his mind. By the end of the summer, it'd seemed as if she'd succeeded.

Until she'd received the call that made it clear she hadn't. She'd stood there stunned long after Max had ended the call. Gutted by a deep, soul-racking pain that had ripped her to shreds.

Eventually, she'd moved on, putting that summer behind her. So why couldn't she look into those dark, brooding eyes without a shiver running down her spine? And why did the timbre of his deep voice still do things to her?

Why didn't matter. She just needed to hold it together for the few months it would take to get this project off the ground. Then they would go their separate ways, and she could put Max Abbott right back where he belonged. In her rearview mirror.

Max sent his last email at the end of what felt like an unbearably long week.

Thankfully, his second meeting with Quinn earlier that morning had gone well. He'd kept their contact during the week minimal and focused on his other projects, allowing Zora and Savannah to bring her up to speed.

The football sponsorship deal was grinding forward, even if it was happening at a snail's pace. And his week had been filled with a series of conference calls. At least he'd gotten a chance to spend some time with his two-year-old nephew, Davis, whom he adored.

Spending time with the precocious little guy was the highlight of any day.

He and Davis had been eating lunch and watching *Bubble Guppies* in the conference room when Savannah had joined them with Quinn in tow.

Quinn had been just as taken with his nephew as he was. Which only made her even more endearing. It'd barely been a week and it seemed that his entire family was enamored with Quinn Bazemore.

Despite being busy with work, he was still preoccupied with thoughts of Quinn.

After all this time, he was as affected by her now as he'd been at twenty-one. When he'd fallen head over heels for her.

Max quietly groaned, thinking of those lush lips and the enticing curve of her hips.

He couldn't pinpoint exactly what it was about Quinn that drove him to distraction. But he was still captivated by her. His heart raced and his pulse quickened when he was around Quinn. And his dreams had been fueled by vivid memories of the intimate moments they'd shared.

"This is more serious than I suspected." Zora startled him when she slid into the chair on the other side of his desk.

"Didn't hear you come in." Max cleared his throat.

"That's because you were in a daze. I called your name twice," she informed him.

"Oh. Well, I was reviewing the day in my head," he stammered.

Zora leaned forward with her elbows on the edge of his desk. "How about we *not* do this thing where you pretend you weren't sitting here thinking about Quinn and let's skip to the part where you tell me what's really going on with you two?"

Max rubbed his jaw and sat back in his chair, narrowing his gaze at the nosiest of his siblings. He'd managed to avoid this conversation all week. Until now. "There's nothing to tell."

"Then why did you freak out when Quinn walked into that conference room?"

"You're being melodramatic. I didn't 'freak out.' I was simply surprised to see—"

"Your ex?" Zora grinned.

"Quinn," he continued, ignoring her accusation. He was prepared to walk the superthin tightrope between lying and just not telling his nosy-ass sister something that clearly wasn't her business. "Because I hadn't seen her in years, and last I heard, she was living in Atlanta."

"So you've been keeping tabs on her since that summer you interned at Bazemore Farms." Zora seemed pleased with herself for extrapolating that bit of information.

"Gramps mentioned it in passing." He shifted his gaze back to his computer and started to shut it down.

"You were floored when you saw Quinn. And you were surprisingly hard on her plan."

"Can you blame me? This project is a big deal. It's Grandpa Joe's way of honoring the last wishes of Savannah's grandfather. Plus, I get the feeling there's a lot riding on this deal for Mr. Bazemore. Maybe you don't feel the pressure of all of those expectations, but I do. So, of course, I'm reluctant to turn the reins for this project over to a virtual stranger."

He shut his laptop and slid it into his bag.

"Quinn isn't a stranger. She's a family friend and an experienced public relations professional. And the way you called her *Peaches*, it felt like you'd had a more intimate relationship." Zora's voice was gentler. "There's no crime in that. But if you still have a thing for her—"

"I don't," he insisted.

Being one of five kids in an outspoken family, it

was par for the course that they gave each other a hard time. But Zora's words had definitely struck a nerve, and they both knew it.

Zora stared at him, neither of them speaking.

Finally, Max spoke. "Look, I know you're just looking out for this deal—"

"And you. Because whether you want to talk about it or not, it's obvious you feel *something* for Quinn. Don't let those feelings cloud your judgment." Zora stood. "Let Quinn work her magic."

Damn his nosy little sister and her insightfulness.

"I won't jeopardize this product launch, Brat. Promise." He'd invoked her childhood nickname, which she liked about as much as Quinn liked Peaches.

"You'd better not." She pointed a finger at him, but then her expression softened. "And be careful, Max. You're in deeper than you realize. You both are."

"Everything is just fine with me and Quinn, I assure you." He stood, lifting his bag onto his shoulder. He'd had enough of his little sister's lecture.

"Great." Zora walked him to the door. "Because I invited Quinn to Mom and Dad's anniversary party."

Max turned to his sister, panic flaring in his chest as he locked the door behind them. "Why?"

"I thought it would make Quinn feel welcome." Zora shrugged. "But she seems reluctant to attend. I think she feels like she'd be crashing our family party. Or maybe she's worried she won't know anyone besides us and her grandfather."

"Then maybe it's better if she doesn't come." Max shrugged as they walked toward Zora's office.

"Or maybe you could invite her," Zora prodded. "I

put you down for a plus-one, but you never did RSVP with one. So there's an extra space beside you that—"

"If I recall, you and Cole have unused plus-ones, too. No one is bothering either of you about it."

"Dallas is coming as my plus-one."

Dallas Hamilton—Zora's best friend since kindergarten—was a self-made millionaire. He'd started his craft furniture business by fiddling with scrap pieces of wood in his family's run-down barn. Despite his mother's best efforts, Dallas and Zora's relationship was still platonic.

"And I know Cole hasn't RSVP'd." It was one of the many things about his youngest brother that irritated him. "That would be far too considerate."

Zora stopped him just outside of her office. "When are you going to stop being so hard on Cole? He chose not to join the family business. So what? You act like he's committed a crime against humanity."

"Grandad created a legacy for *all* of us." Max waved his hand around the impressive office space that had been expanded and remodeled over the years. "But Cole just blew it off. He's always felt the need to buck the system."

"Yes, Cole is doing his own thing, and he's damn good at it. It's obviously the thing he was meant to do."

"That isn't the point."

"Isn't it? Because what Grandad wants for us more than anything is that we're happy and successful in life. Cole has found that. He's the premier home builder in the area. Why can't you just be happy for him?" Zora poked a sharp finger into his bicep that would likely leave one hell of a bruise.

Maybe he deserved it.

"Ready to shut it down? If so, I'll walk you to your car." The shift in topic was his clear signal that their discussion about Cole was over.

Max leaned against the door frame while his sister gathered her things. He toyed with her suggestion to invite Quinn to his parents' anniversary party.

A part of him wanted to spend time with Quinn socially. But the part of his brain that was fully functioning when it came to Quinn Bazemore recognized that it was a horrible idea.

"You should reconsider inviting Quinn to the party," Zora said as they left the building and headed into the executive parking lot. "We're working on a really short timeline on this project. You two need to be in sync, and you need to learn to trust each other. This party is the perfect opportunity for you to get reacquainted in a relaxed setting."

"No, Zora," he said firmly as they arrived at his sister's car. "End of discussion." He folded his arms and stared down his scheming little sister, who was clearly amused by his resistance to her not-so-subtle matchmaking.

She squeezed the car door handle and the doors unlocked. "I reserve the right to resume this line of questioning at a later date."

There was that one year of law school Zora had taken, rearing its head again.

"And I reserve the right to ignore it." Max gave his sister a one-armed hug. "Good night, Brat. Drive safe."

Zora laughed as she slung her bags into the back seat and slid in behind the wheel. "You, too."

Max shook his head as he watched his sister drive off. Then he walked toward his SUV.

The only other person as invested in his love life as his sister was their mother. Iris Abbott had been trying to marry her kids off since long before Savannah had arrived in town.

But with Blake married to Savannah, Parker engaged to Kayleigh, and their second grandchild on the way, his mother had eased off on pressuring the rest of them.

Zora was obviously still on mission—as long as she wasn't the person being matched.

Six

Quinn stepped out of her car and handed her keys to the valet. She smoothed down the front of the floor-length, pale blue, one-shoulder Marchesa gown that she'd blown a mint on and had never gotten to wear.

She lifted the hem of the dress so it wouldn't drag on the ground. Quinn felt slightly ridiculous walking into a barn in a floor-length gown with a small train. But Zora had stipulated that the event was black-tie, and this was the only dress she'd brought to Knoxville that seemed dressy enough for it.

"You look beautiful, sweetheart." Her grandfather extended his arm. "If your grandmother could see how much you look like her right now." He chuckled softly. "She'd be pleased as punch."

"Thanks, Gramps." She sucked in a quiet breath and surveyed the large building with its weathered exterior. Bright, festive strings of fairy lights adorned the top of the structure, providing a warm contrast to the cool gray exterior. Strings of hanging white bulbs led up the pathway to the open barn door.

The decor inside was simply breathtaking. Glamorous, but with a nod to the rustic surroundings. Swaths of cream-colored fabric hung from the ceiling, as did several beautiful chandeliers. The tables were draped in rich, sumptuous fabrics. Yet the centerpieces and table decorations evoked the mountains and the nature that surrounded them.

Mason jars of various sizes were adorned with burlap and lace and overflowing with small bouquets of flowers. The table runners were accented with sprawling greenery that ran the length of each table. There were glass bottles in a kaleidoscope of colors and lanterns filled with candles all throughout the space. And the chair backs were topped by chiffon hoods in a dusty rose with ruffled embellishments.

"This place is incredible, Gramps. Did Savannah do all of this?" It was a visual feast.

"She sure did. Before Savannah came along, this was just a run-down barn—a little too rustic." Her grandfather chuckled. "Since the renovation and decor upgrade, they've easily tripled their event income." He nodded in Savannah's direction. "She's a savvy businesswoman, and so are you. You'll show 'em."

"Thanks, Gramps." She squeezed his arm. He always seemed to know when she needed a shot of confidence.

A woman whom Quinn recognized from Savannah's staff took their names and gave them their table assignments.

After they greeted a few of her grandfather's

friends, they parted ways. Quinn pressed a fist to the knot in her stomach. Suddenly she wished she'd taken Zora up on her offer to rearrange the seating chart so she could sit with her grandfather.

But the truth was she wouldn't be here if it hadn't been for the series of frantic text messages she'd received last night.

I need a plus-one for my parents' anniversary party.

To which she'd responded, I'm sure you'll have no problem finding someone.

True. LOL. But this is a family event, so I'd rather hang out with someone I have zero interest in.

Your "bedside" manner sucks. No wonder you can't find a date.

Also true. You should take pity on me.

This was followed by the Puss in Boots puppy dog eyes GIF.

Not fair! You know I can't resist a good Shrek GIF!

Besides, there'll be free food and booze plus party favors. And my charming company, of course. Come. PLEASE.

I'm thinking you got in line twice when egos were handed out. But the free food and booze sounds tempting. What kind of party favors are we talking?

Guess you'll have to come to find out.

She hadn't responded, but on the third, increasingly desperate request, she'd given in. The texts had made her laugh, plus she was half-asleep by then, so she'd let her guard down and accepted the invitation. But as she scanned the open space, she didn't see Mr. It's-Definitely-Not-A-Date anywhere.

"Quinn, you look gorgeous." Savannah said as she approached, wearing a long, flowing, wrap gown in a sumptuous red fabric. A sash was tied just above her belly. Her hair was braided in an elaborate updo that completed the goddess look. "I didn't realize you'd changed your mind about coming tonight."

"It was a *really* last-minute decision." Quinn fought back the urge to touch her hair and make sure her hasty updo was still in place. "I hope it's okay that I'm here."

"Of course, it is." Savannah nodded at someone over Quinn's shoulder and held up her index finger before turning back to her. "I have to take care of a few things before we get started, but I trust that you know where you're seated?"

"I do. Go. We'll catch up later." Quinn's hands trembled slightly as she surveyed the room filled with people. "I could use some of that free booze right about now," she muttered under her breath as she moved toward the bar at the back of the room.

"Quinn, you came after all." Zora gave her a genuine hug that eased some of the tension in her shoulders. "I didn't realize you'd changed your mind."

"Your brother is persuasive and persistent," Quinn said.

Zora's eyes lit up. "Well, good for him. I'm glad

he was able to talk you into joining us." She scanned the crowd, then waved at someone on the other side of the room.

Quinn turned to the bartender and ordered a glass of white wine. When she turned around again, she met a familiar stare.

"Hey." Max's gaze drifted down the length of her body before returning to her face.

"Good evening, Max." Beneath his stare, Quinn felt self-conscious in the dress, which exposed her back, one shoulder and a bit of cleavage. "You look… handsome."

"Thanks." He smoothed down his beautiful purple necktie—the perfect complement to his white shirt and charcoal-gray tuxedo, accented by a purple pocket square. "And you look…incredible." Max gestured toward her, then cleared his throat. "But I'm surprised to see you here. Zora said you passed on the invite."

"What do you mean you're surprised to see her here?" Zora gave Max the strangest look. "Quinn said you invited her."

"No, *I* invited her." As Cole joined them, he signaled for the bartender to give him a refill, then set his empty glass on the bar and leaned in to give Quinn a bear hug. Finally, he released her. "Thanks for rescuing me tonight. I know it was last-minute. I owe you one."

"Cole, *you* invited Quinn?" Zora's eyes went wide.

"Who else would've invited her?" Cole gave Zora a quick hug and acknowledged Max with a slight head nod.

Zora stared at Cole, then shifted her attention to Quinn. "I didn't realize that you two were—"

"Friends," Quinn volunteered quickly, so there

would be no misunderstandings. "Cole and I became friends about four years ago. We ran into each other in Atlanta one weekend when Cole was in town visiting friends."

"Wow. I did *not* know that. Did you, Max?" Zora elbowed her brother, who was staring at the two of them as if Quinn had just declared that they'd been abducted by aliens.

"Uh...no," Max said, still staring at her. He turned to his brother. "Cole, how is it that you never mentioned that you and Mr. Bazemore's granddaughter were such good friends?"

So now I've been bumped down to "Mr. Bazemore's granddaughter." Fine.

The more distance between them the easier it would be for them to work together for the next few months.

Cole thanked the bartender for his drink and shoved money in the glass tip jar.

"Just never came up, I guess." He shrugged. "Funny story, though. Quinn and I hooked up at a speed dating event."

Oh, God. He had to tell the story, didn't he?

"You two dated?" Deep grooves formed across Max's forehead.

"No, we did *not*." Quinn paused, allowing that clear statement to sink in before continuing. She shot her friend a warning look and Cole smirked. Quinn turned back to Max and Zora. "*Hooked up* probably isn't the best word choice. Once we started talking, we each recognized who the other was and—"

"She shut me down immediately." Cole chuckled, as if the concept of a woman not being interested in him romantically was remarkable. "What was it that you said exactly?"

Quinn's cheeks stung under the heat of Max's and Zora's stares. She sighed quietly. "I believe I told you that you had a better chance of being hit by a meteorite than you did of getting me into bed."

Cole laughed as hard as he had the night she'd said it. She and Zora couldn't help laughing, too. But Max clearly wasn't amused by their friendship meet-cute.

"I knew right then that we were going to be friends. After the event, we went to this amazing burger joint, then we went out dancing. It was honestly the best time I'd ever had in Atlanta." Cole draped an arm over her shoulder. "Since then, we've kept in touch."

"I'm impressed, Quinn. You're probably my brother's first platonic female friend since middle school," Zora said. "Maybe there's hope for you after all, Cole." She slipped her arm through Max's. "Well, there are a few things we should take care of before the festivities start. Excuse us."

Zora, in her elegant white jumpsuit with a low-cut back, guided Max to the other side of the barn. Quinn couldn't miss the tension in his jaw and shoulders or the narrowing of his gaze as he glanced back at her.

Did Max honestly have the nerve to be angry about her friendship with Cole?

She certainly wasn't trying to make him jealous by being here with his brother. Cole had blown up her phone with text messages, asking her to be his guest for the event. And they were *just* friends.

Max watched his mother practically float through the room after the big surprise reveal. The presentation had begun with all of the siblings sharing some of their parents' history as a couple. Then they'd shared some of their favorite parenting stories. But then his brother Parker's fiancée came out to deliver the big surprise. King's Finest had purchased Kayleigh Jemison's building as a gift to their mother, Iris.

The building, home to Kayleigh's jewelry design business and consignment shop, was once owned by his mother's family. They'd run a small, family-style restaurant there until it had gone out of business when Max's maternal grandfather had been swindled out of a bundle of cash and he lost the place.

Their mother had mused about opening a family restaurant in memory of her father's legacy. As a surprise to her on her wedding anniversary, the Abbotts had decided to fulfill their mother's dream by buying the building and turning it into a family restaurant associated with the distillery.

The unexpected bonus was that Kayleigh and Parker had resolved a decades-long feud and become engaged during the course of the negotiations.

It had been surreal to see how moved Parker— who rarely exhibited emotion—was over Kayleigh's speech. And how tenderly he'd hugged and kissed his fiancée when she was done.

Max would've bet the house that Parker would end up as that crotchety old uncle who never married and yelled at the neighborhood kids to get off his lawn. But now he and Kayleigh were engaged, and Kayleigh had moved into Parker's house with her golden retriever—whom Parker doted on.

It was a shocking turn of events no one in their family had seen coming.

Cole would clearly be the old player who chose not to marry. He'd still be dating half the women at the nursing home at ninety.

So maybe Max had been demoted to eternal, grouchy bachelor status. Standing alone in the corner, scowling, he was off to a great start.

From where he stood, he could easily see Quinn.

"You okay, big brother?" Zora handed him a glass of punch.

"Why wouldn't I be?" he asked after thanking her for the drink.

"Because you evidently feel something for Quinn and now… Well, she's here with Cole instead. Which wouldn't have happened had you asked her yourself, like I suggested."

Max gritted his teeth, wishing he'd taken his sister's advice. Still, he wouldn't admit as much to Zora. It would only further encourage her to stick her nose where it didn't belong.

"Quinn and I are coworkers, just like we were the summer I interned at the farm," he said. *True*. "And she has every right to be here with her grandfather, Cole, or anyone else on the guest list." Max shrugged. "It's none of my business, *or yours*, who Quinn is seeing."

"Then why are you standing here lightweight stalking her?" Zora shook a finger to head off his objection. "Not up for debate. I saw you watching them just now."

Shit. Had he become *that* guy? The one who didn't know when to let go and move on?

Zora carefully sipped the red punch so she wouldn't

get it on her white jumpsuit. "Are you buying this story about Cole and Quinn just being friends?"

Max sucked in a quiet breath, then sighed. "I hope so. Because if there's more to it and Cole screws up and upsets her, he could throw a wrench into this whole operation. There's a lot at stake here for all of us."

"I know," Zora agreed. "But if they are together, I'm happy for them. I just hate that it'll make you unhappy."

Max draped an arm over his sister's shoulder and sighed. He appreciated her support, even if it would be wiser not to say so. He glanced over to where Cole and Quinn had been sitting, but they were gone. Where they'd gone was none of his business.

"C'mon, Brat. We should check in with Mom and Dad."

"Mom and Dad are fine. They're showing off out on the dance floor. We should join them." She put down her punch and his, then tugged him onto the dance floor without waiting for his response.

Max followed his sister. This was a celebration of his mother and father's forty amazing years of marriage and the incredible family that had resulted from it, for which he was grateful.

Time to stop pouting and at least make a show of having a good time.

Today was about his parents, not him and his regrets.

Seven

Quinn had danced with Cole, her grandfather and his stable of widowed or divorced friends. The sparkly four-inch, open-toe sandals she was wearing were killing her feet and she was pretty sure there would be indentions from the straps across her instep. But it had been an amazing night.

She'd worried that she would feel like an intruder during this momentous occasion. Instead, the Abbotts made everyone in the room feel like they were family. It'd been a lovely evening filled with love. But what had stayed with her most was Kayleigh's speech.

I am so grateful to have my best friend and the love of my life back. I'm thankful that we were able to break down the wall we'd erected between us. That we didn't allow our misguided pride to keep us from the thing we needed most: each other.

When Kayleigh said the words, tears had filled Quinn's eyes and her focus had shifted involuntarily to Max, who met her gaze.

Had Kayleigh's words made him think of her, too?

"Lost in thought?" Cole, her dance partner, leaned in to be heard over the music.

"I was thinking about Kayleigh's speech."

"It was beautiful, huh? I'll admit, she *almost* got me." He chuckled, nodding toward Parker and his fiancée dancing together. "I'm thrilled for them."

"They seem happy and incredibly in love." Quinn stole one more glance at the couple. Kayleigh's curly red hair was twisted up in a bun with a few curls hanging free.

"Switch partners?" Zora asked. She was dancing beside them.

Quinn studied Max's face. He looked as mortified by the prospect as she felt. This obviously wasn't his idea.

"If Quinn doesn't mind." Cole looked to her.

She took a step backward and her heel caught in the hem of her dress. Before she could fall and make a scene, Max was there, his arms encircling her waist.

"I've got it from here." Max's gaze locked with hers.

Quinn nodded to let Cole know she was okay with the switch. She and Max danced together in silence for a few moments before she finally spoke.

"Thank you. My shoe got caught in the back of my dress."

"I noticed." Max's tone was flat and unreadable. "You didn't twist your ankle, did you?"

"No. Just battered my pride." Her face still stung with embarrassment over the near miss.

"Have I told you how amazing you look tonight?" he asked after a beat of silence between them.

"You have." Quinn couldn't help the slow smile that tightened her cheeks. "But it's just as nice hearing it the second time."

Max leaned down and whispered in her ear. "Good. Because it bears repeating. You look sensational."

Quinn's cheeks and chest warmed. She gave silent thanks for the melanin that masked the flush of her skin. Especially in a dimly lit room like this one. But she had no mechanism to disguise the erratic beating of her heart, which Max could no doubt feel through his fingertips pressed to her back.

"Thank you." One of her hands rested on his upper arm. Even through the fabric of his tailored tux, she could feel the impressive bicep. "But why do I feel like I'm not going to like whatever you're about to say next?"

Max halted momentarily. Tilting his head, he studied her. He lowered their joined hands and resumed their movement. His posture stiffened.

"This thing with you and Cole…"

"You mean my *friendship* with Cole," she corrected him. Now her body tensed. "What of it?"

"Seems odd that neither of you have mentioned it before."

Tension trailed up her shoulders and into her jaw. "And when exactly would I have shared that with you, Max? Before this week, we haven't seen or talked to each other in years."

"I realize that, Quinn, and you may not want to

hear it, but I regret that. I regret *how* things ended," he clarified.

"So you don't regret unceremoniously dumping me, just that you were a jerk about it." She met his gaze. "Got it."

"It's not that simple, Quinn." He frowned. After a few moments of uncomfortable silence, he said, "We met twice this week. You didn't mention your friendship with Cole either time."

"I didn't mention any of my other friends, my parents or my siblings, either," she noted calmly. "Because those weren't social meetings. They were business meetings, so we discussed business. Because despite this dance, that's the extent of our relationship."

She stopped, extracting herself from his grip. "Thank you for the dance, but it's been a long night and I have a long drive ahead of me. It's time I say good-night to everyone."

"Quinn, I didn't mean to upset you." He lightly gripped her wrist, pinning her in place. "Wouldn't you be suspicious if I'd showed up at your office in Atlanta and claimed to have a four-year-long friendship with your younger sister?" His pleading tone begged her to be reasonable. "Wouldn't you find that *odd*?"

"Why is it so hard for you to believe that my relationship with Cole is purely platonic? Do you sleep with *every* woman you meet?" She yanked her arm from his grip.

"No, but my brother does." He folded his arms over his broad chest. "Or didn't Cole mention that?"

"Maybe your brother isn't prepared to get involved in a long-term monogamous relationship. But at least he communicates openly and honestly with the women he's involved with. Call me old-fashioned, but I admire that in a man, whether he's a friend or a lover."

Max cringed when she used the word *lover*. It seemed that the very thought of her and Cole together evoked a physical reaction.

If she were a better person, perhaps she wouldn't have taken the slightest bit of delight in the discomfort the thought evidently caused him.

"You don't know my brother the way I do, Quinn. He doesn't do relationships. Whatever this is between you two…he's only going to hurt you."

"Maybe you don't know your brother as well as you think you do." She poked a finger in his chest and did her best not to react to the firm muscles she encountered. Instead, she focused on being indignant on her friend's behalf. "Cole's right. You underestimate him and you don't respect his choices. That's a shame. Because despite everything, he still looks up to his big brothers, including you."

"I'm sure Cole has made me the bad guy in all this, but—"

"Do you honestly think we spend our time together discussing you?" Quinn asked with a humorless laugh. "Spoiler alert—we don't. Get over yourself, Max."

Quinn made her way across the crowded dance floor and returned to the table where her grandfather and most of the Abbott family were assembled.

She forced a smile and slid into the seat beside her grandfather. Leaning in closer so that only he could hear her, she asked, "Ready to head out? We have a long drive home."

"Actually, there's been a change of plans." He

smiled. "The celebration continues tomorrow with brunch at Duke and Iris's place. You and I are invited. Then Joe and I are going fishing tomorrow afternoon with a few friends."

"You're driving all the way back here tomorrow morning?" Looking at her wrist, she checked the thin, delicate antique watch that had once belonged to her grandmother. "It's already so late."

"Which is why I'm staying in one of Joe's spare rooms at the cabin. Don't worry, he's got an extra room for you."

Spend the night with Gramps at his buddy's bachelor pad? Hard pass.

"That's generous of Grandpa Joe," Quinn said. "But I don't want to encroach on your buddy time. I'll just drive back to Knoxville tonight and come back and get you tomorrow afternoon, after you guys have gone fishing. I'll bring the cooler."

"You're not coming to brunch?" Cole slid into the empty seat on the other side of Quinn. He set a small mason jar of peach cobbler and a sculpted glass bowl filled with vanilla ice cream in front of her. "You should definitely come to brunch. The spread is going to be amazing."

Warm peach cobbler and homemade vanilla ice cream?

Cole knew her weakness and was prepared to play dirty. She stared at the cobbler but didn't touch either dish.

"Listen to Cole, sweetheart." Her grandfather got up from his chair and patted Cole on the shoulder before sauntering back onto the dance floor at the invitation of an insistent older woman Quinn didn't recognize.

"Your grandad is right." Cole nudged her with his shoulder. "You should come to brunch tomorrow."

"It sounds nice," Quinn admitted. He handed her a spoon, and she broke down and tried a little of the miniature cobbler with a spoonful of the ice cream. "That's really good."

Not *quite* as good as hers, but still delicious.

"I'm pretty sure there'll be more at brunch tomorrow," he teased in a singsong voice as he dug into a small mason jar of apple crisp.

"By the time I get back to Knoxville tonight, it'll be really late. Then I'll have turn around and come right back here."

"So stay here," he said, as if the solution should be evident.

"I'm not up for a sleepover with our grandfathers at Grandpa Joe's cabin," she muttered through another spoonful of food.

"Don't knock it till you've tried it. Give those two a bottle of top-shelf bourbon and they'll tell you anything you want to know. Actually, way more than you ever wanted to know or can mentally unsee." Cole chuckled.

"That's gross and it proves my point." She nearly choked on her cobbler, laughing. "I'll pass."

Savannah, Blake, Parker and Kayleigh, who'd all evidently tuned into her and Cole's conversation, burst into laughter, too.

"Sounds like Gramps and Mr. B," Blake said.

"So don't stay with the notorious GPs." Cole shrugged, using his and Quinn's shared nickname for their grandfathers. He took another bite of apple crisp. "Stay at my place instead."

There was a collective gasp at the table, which Cole was either oblivious to or chose to ignore.

Maybe she misunderstood him.

"Do you have a rental place in town?" Quinn knew that Cole owned property at the beach in Charleston, but he'd never mentioned having local property aside from his home.

"No. But I do have a guest room, and you're welcome to it." He shoved another spoonful of apple crisp into his mouth, blissfully ignorant that everyone at the table was staring.

"Or you could stay with me. I have a spare guest room, too," Zora offered.

Cole finally seemed to notice he had everyone's attention. He shrugged. "My place is closer."

"She's *not* staying at your place, Cole." The entire table turned toward the source of the gruff voice. Max stood behind them, his hands clenched at his sides.

"As long as she's safe—and she will be—why the hell do you care where Quinn sleeps tonight?" Cole glanced over his shoulder at Max. His expression was neutral, despite the tension evident in his tone. "Who died and made you either of our fathers?"

"No one thinks they're anyone's daddy." Zora glanced cautiously between her brothers. "I think maybe Max just feels Quinn might be more comfortable staying with someone—"

"She barely knows?" Cole raised an eyebrow.

Everyone at the table turned to look at her. Quinn's face was heated as she glanced around. Max was fit to be tied. Cole seemed to straddle the line between being mildly annoyed and gleefully irking his brother. Zora seemed desperate to play peacemaker. Savannah, Blake, Kayleigh and Parker were all riveted by the conversation, as if they were watching a messy reality TV drama.

Quinn stood suddenly, careful not to trip on her dress this time. "Thank you both for the invitation. I don't want to inconvenience either of you. It would probably be best if I just headed home."

"I have a suggestion," Kayleigh spoke up, drawing everyone's attention. "I do have a rental unit in town. Now that the building officially belongs to King's Finest, I won't be renting out the unit anymore. Construction doesn't begin for at least another month, right, Cole?" She looked at her future brother-in-law for confirmation. He nodded begrudgingly. "So why don't you stay there tonight, Quinn?"

"That's a great idea, babe." Parker squeezed her hand. "In fact, the place is just going to be sitting empty for the next month. So you're welcome to use the place rather than commuting back and forth to Knoxville every day."

"That's an excellent idea, Parker," Zora said. Blake and Savannah agreed.

"You're sure?" Quinn was still on the fence about spending the night in Magnolia Lake. However, using the place as a crash pad for the next month would be ideal. The drive back and forth each day was exhausting. "I'd have to pay you, of course."

"No, you don't," Blake insisted. "Like Kayleigh said, it would just be sitting empty."

"But not the entire building," Kayleigh clarified. "My shop is on the first floor, and we won't be moving it for a few weeks." Parker's fiancée pulled a pen out of her crystal-studded Alexander McQueen clutch with its signature skull and knuckle-duster clasp. She scribbled on a napkin, then folded it and passed it to Parker, who handed it to Quinn.

There was an address and two six-number codes.

"The building and the apartment have key code locks. That's all you'll need to get in. I can walk you through the place if you'd like," Kayleigh said.

"No, I'll be fine. Thank you, Kayleigh."

"Will you need clothes? I'm sure I have something you could borrow. We could swing by my place and take a look," Zora offered.

"I have a change of clothing in my workout bag in the trunk, but thank you, Zora," Quinn said absently.

I guess I'm really doing this.

With her overnight arrangements settled, the conversation returned to its normal ebb and flow. But as Max took his seat, there was still a hint of tension between him and Cole.

"You're not upset that I passed on staying with you, are you?" Quinn whispered, nudging Cole.

"No, of course not. I'm just glad you'll be at brunch tomorrow." He flashed that million-dollar smile, the one she could never resist reciprocating. "I have to do something for my dad, but I'll be ready to leave in an hour or so. If you don't mind waiting that long, I'd be happy to do a walk-through with you at Kayleigh's place."

"No need. I'm exhausted, so I'm leaving in a bit. Thanks anyway."

"Then text me once you're settled, so I know you're okay." Cole hugged her, then left the table.

Max peered at her for a moment, then got up and left the table, too.

Quinn sighed softly.

You don't owe him an explanation. Just let it go.

But the hurt look on Max's face tugged at her chest for reasons she couldn't explain. Or maybe she could. But the truth was simply too painful to bear.

Eight

"Cole!" Max hadn't meant to call his brother so loudly, but he was seething with anger as he waited patiently for Cole to finish talking to their parents.

Cole glanced at him and rolled his eyes before stalking over. He folded his arms, his legs planted wide.

"What is it now, Max? Is this our quarterly conversation where you accuse me of being a self-interested ingrate who isn't toeing the family line?"

"Can we talk?" Max refused to acknowledge his brother's flippant remark.

"Isn't that what we're doing?" Cole raised a brow.

"Privately," Max said. He turned and walked toward the back office, near the restrooms. Max used his keys to open the door and they went inside.

"Are you deliberately trying to sabotage this deal

with Bazemore Farms?" Max sat on the front edge of the desk.

"Why on earth would you ask a dumbass question like that?" Cole's nostrils flared.

Max forced himself not to react to his brother's raised voice. "Then let me rephrase the question. What the hell is going on with you and Quinn?"

"First, I don't see how that's any of your business. Second, Quinn was pretty clear about it. She and I are friends. We have been for a few years."

"You never mentioned being friends with Dixon Bazemore's granddaughter. Not once." Now Max's voice was slightly elevated.

"I didn't mention it to you," Cole said. "But then our conversations pretty much consist of *this*. You calling me on the carpet like I'm still twelve. I'm not. I'm thirty-three fucking years old, Max. And last I heard, Duke and Iris Abbott are my parents. Not you." He jabbed a finger in his direction.

Max ground his back teeth, his muscles tensing. He and Cole were what his late grandmother referred to as Irish twins, born just under twelve months apart.

Yet, Cole and Zora had always been closer.

"Maybe try not acting like a horny teenager all the time," Max said. "Show a little self-control, as adults do. Like by not taking every single woman you meet to bed. Especially when she's the granddaughter of Grandpa Joe's closest living friend."

Projecting much?

Yep, he was a total hypocrite for that one.

If he got taken out by a lightning strike right this moment, he couldn't even complain. He legit had it coming.

"I am *not* sleeping with Quinn." Cole stabbed his finger angrily at the air in front of Max's face. "Because, as I already told you, she shot me down. I respected her decision then, as I do now. I haven't made a move on her since then."

"Really? Because you two seem *overly* familiar. You keep putting your hands on her. Hugging her. Whispering in her ear. Draping your arm over her shoulder."

"Is that what you've been doing all night? Spying on me and Quinn? Dude, you seriously need to get a life…or get laid. Maybe both." Cole smirked in a way that made Max want to grab him by the collar.

"I have a life. And right now, this joint brandy project with Bazemore Farms is at the center of it. So I need you to back off of Quinn before you blow up the entire deal and cause irreparable damage to Gramps's relationship with Dixon Bazemore," Max said.

"I realize you always think the worst of me," Cole said. A hint of anger and maybe hurt glinted in his brother's dark eyes. "But Quinn told you herself we're just friends. Are you calling her a liar, too?"

"It's not that I think the worst of you, Cole. It's that I expect better. Being an Abbott means something, you know."

"You don't think I know that?" Cole laughed bitterly. "None of you ever let me forget it. But you don't get to define what being an Abbott means for me," he said without a hint of apology. "Now, you want to tell me what this is really about? Because this is extra, even for you."

Cole's voice faded at the end of the sentence and

then his eyes widened with realization. He rubbed his chin. "Oh."

"Oh…what?" Max asked casually, despite the subtle quickening of his pulse.

"I've seen this movie before. You're into Quinn. That's why you want me to back off." Cole paced the floor. He stopped, then turned to him abruptly. "No, it's more than that. That summer you worked at Bazemore Farms… The two of you were together, weren't you? *That's* why Quinn shut everything down between us the moment she realized I was your brother."

Max closed his eyes. His cheeks and forehead burned with heat.

Seriously, you had one job, asshole.

He'd promised to keep his relationship with Quinn under wraps. That he'd *never* kiss and tell. Even if she hadn't kept her side of the bargain, it'd been important to him that he kept his promise to her. But watching Cole with Quinn all night… His jealousy had circumvented his better judgment.

What conclusion did he expect Cole to come to after his full-court press about his brother's relationship with Quinn?

Cole was a lot of things. Stupid wasn't one of them.

"You've been spending too much time with Zora," Max said. "I'm just trying to protect our family's interest here. Something you seem to care very little about."

Flames seemed to shoot from Cole's dark eyes as he stepped forward, his hands clenched at his side.

"This isn't about me or this brandy deal. It's about you wanting Quinn. I'm guessing you screwed up with her back then."

Max wouldn't look at Cole, unwilling to confirm or deny his brother's accusation.

"First, Parker thinks I'm making a move on Kayleigh. Now you think I'm screwing Quinn. News flash—I'm *not* that guy. You'd think my own damn brothers would realize that."

Max raised his head and met Cole's intense stare. There was genuine pain in his brother's voice and expression.

Guilt churned in Max's gut. "You're right. Quinn and I were involved back when I worked on the farm. No one else knows."

Max's head spun with all of the complicated emotions he'd felt for Quinn that summer. Emotions he'd buried and thought were long dead until Quinn Bazemore sashayed into that conference room earlier that week and turned his world upside down. It had unearthed a complicated mixture of feelings: affection, admiration, desire, love, guilt and pain.

"But this isn't about how you felt about her back then, is it? You're still into her." There was pity in Cole's voice rather than the resentment that had been there moments earlier. When Max didn't respond, Cole added, "Let me help you out—that wasn't a question."

"I'm not discussing this with you," Max said.

"And I'm tired of you guys projecting your bullshit on me." Cole shoved a finger in his direction again. "If you want another shot with Quinn, man up and tell her. If you're not willing to do that, then leave her the fuck alone. Because you never deserved her anyway."

Max had no argument. Quinn did deserve better.

"Quinn is special, Max. I don't have many friends

like her. So make up with her. Don't make up with her. Whatever. But I won't give up my friendship with Quinn just because you're pissed that you screwed things up with her a lifetime ago. So get your head outta your ass and either shoot your shot or get over it. *Period*."

Cole left the office, slamming the door behind him.

Max closed his eyes and heaved a sigh. God, he hated it when Cole was right.

He sucked in a deep breath, his mind buzzing with all of the things he'd wanted to say to Quinn and all the reasons he shouldn't say them. Starting with the fact that she clearly didn't want to hear them.

Quinn wouldn't even let him apologize. So how could he possibly tell her the truth? That he'd never stopped caring for her. That he'd do anything to hit Rewind and do things differently.

She wasn't ready to hear his truth, and he had no right to impose it on her to assuage his own guilt. He'd screwed up, so he had to take the L.

The words of his high school football coach echoed in his head.

Don't force it, son. Read the field and take whatever the defense gives you.

That was exactly what he needed to do.

Stop behaving like a possessive asshole and accept the small olive branch Quinn has extended.

He needed to find Quinn now.

Nine

Quinn handed her ticket to the valet, and the man left to retrieve her car. Suddenly a familiar voice called her name.

She turned to find Max jogging toward her with an intense look on his face.

Her heart raced. "Is my grandfather okay?"

"Sorry, I didn't mean to alarm you. Mr. B is fine. I just…" He cleared his throat, then shoved his hands into his pants pockets. "You're not familiar with the area, and since half the town is here tonight, downtown will be pretty deserted."

"I don't expect I'll have any problem finding the place," Quinn said.

"Still, I would feel better if someone…" He cleared his throat again. "I would feel better if I saw you home and made sure everything was okay." He straightened out his cuff links.

"Are you concerned about my safety, Max? Or are you worried that I'll meet up with Cole afterward?" Quinn folded her arms, irritated that Max obviously didn't believe there was nothing going on between her and his brother.

"I'm concerned about you, of course." He lightly gripped her elbow and guided her to a spot a few feet away from the valet stand where the two remaining valets had turned their attention toward them. "About earlier, what I said about you and Cole. I'm sorry. I was way out of line. Forgive me?"

She studied the handsome features that had always intrigued her and the dark, piercing eyes that stared back at her. Eyes she'd gotten lost in many a night during that long, hot summer.

Quinn released a quiet sigh and nodded. "Okay."

"Okay, you forgive me for being an ass earlier? Or okay, I can see you to Kayleigh's place tonight?"

"Both." One side of her mouth curved in an involuntary smile. "But I'm leaving now. Don't you need to be here until the end of the party?"

"I'll come back after I see you home." He dug his valet ticket out of his inside jacket pocket and handed it to the valet. "Pull out to the edge of the property and wait. Then you can follow me into town."

"Okay," Quinn agreed.

When the valet returned with her car, she reached into her purse to tip the kid, but Max waved her off and tipped him generously. She thanked him, then drove to the edge of the property and waited.

A small part of her was eager to be alone with

Max in that apartment. The same part of her that had relished being in his arms again on that dance floor.

Max was her distant past. That crazy, hot summer they shared was a fantasy they'd both awakened from once they'd returned to the reality of their daily lives.

He'd obviously put it out of his mind. Why couldn't she do the same?

Maybe because what they'd shared had evidently meant more to her than it had to him. Max was her first love, and she'd fallen hard for him.

She'd been so sure they'd shared a deep, unbreakable bond. But Max had forgotten her the moment he'd put her grandfather's farm in the rearview mirror.

She should take notes and do the same.

They could work together. Be friendly. Even share an occasional dance. But she wasn't a starry-eyed eighteen-year-old anymore. She understood how the world worked. That people didn't always mean what they said…what they promised. Not even the people who'd promised to love you.

Quinn's attention was drawn to the headlights that flashed in her side view mirror. Max pulled beside her in his SUV and indicated she should follow him. She did, though she'd already plugged the address into her phone's GPS app.

They went back past the distillery, then followed the undulating road to a one-lane bridge that led them into downtown Magnolia Lake. Max pulled his black SUV into a parking lot next to an older block of buildings. She parked beside him as he rummaged for something in the back of his truck.

Their cars were the only two in the lot. Suddenly Quinn was grateful Max had insisted on seeing her here. The area did feel deserted. And aside from the dim lighting in the front window of Kayleigh's store, the building looked abandoned.

Quinn grabbed her gym bag from the trunk and slammed it shut, then gathered the bottom of her dress in her other hand, not wanting a repeat of her earlier clumsiness.

Max had what looked like a T-shirt draped over his shoulder. He reached for her bag.

"I've got it," she insisted.

"Your hands are already full." He indicated where she held up the hem of her dress. "And I don't mind. Really."

Quinn handed the bag off to him as they moved toward the side entrance of the building. From her bag she retrieved the napkin with the codes and punched in the six digits for the main door.

Max opened the heavy door and they stepped inside. The sound of her heels clicking against the wooden floor echoed in the narrow stairwell. When they reached the apartment door, Quinn entered the next six-digit code. The decor in the cozy little one-bedroom apartment was absolutely adorable. Nothing extravagant, but the kind of place she could easily imagine spending the next few weeks.

They walked through the space, and Max dropped Quinn's gym bag at the foot of the bed.

"That reminds me," he said. "If you need anything, Zora said give her a call. I assume you have her cell number."

"I do."

Quinn tossed her clutch on the bed and released the bobby pins in her hair that had been killing her all night. She shook her hair loose and raked her fingers through it, sighing with relief. When she looked up, Max was staring at her.

"Is there anything else?" Quinn asked.

"No." Max shook his head and took a step backward. "Actually...yes." He snatched the garment he was carrying off his shoulder. "I had a clean T-shirt in my gym bag. I thought you might need something to sleep in."

He held out a white T-shirt with the words King's Finest Distillery, Magnolia Lake, Tennessee printed on it in black lettering.

"Thank you." She accepted it, noticing how the soft, cotton had already taken on a subtle hint of Max's cologne.

They stood in silence, the air around them heavy with all of the words that neither of them would allow themselves to say.

For the briefest moment, she wished Max would lean down and kiss her. Satisfy her growing curiosity.

Had his kiss really been as amazing as she remembered? Or had she just been a misguided young woman with so little experience that any kiss would've seemed memorable?

Max's phone rang. Heaving a quiet sigh, he pulled the phone from his inside pocket and checked the caller ID before sliding it back into place. His expression was unreadable.

Was it a woman calling him this late in the evening?

After all, if it had been a member of his family, wouldn't he have answered the phone, as he had many times before in her presence?

So what if some woman was calling him at Netflix-and-chill hour? What business was it of hers?

"I have to go," Max said. "Lock up after me."

Quinn followed Max back through the apartment wondering about the identity of his mystery caller.

Was it someone she'd met at the party tonight? Someone who worked at the distillery? Or maybe someone who lived nearby? Maybe that was the real reason he left the party early.

"Good night, Quinn." His intense gaze shot straight through her, sending tingles down her spine and heating her skin. "Guess I'll see you tomorrow."

"At noon, right?" she asked, then added, "Wait, I don't know where we're meeting for brunch."

"At my parents' place. It's at the end of the same road where the barn is. I'll text the address to you." He pulled out his phone and tapped on the screen.

"You have my cell phone number?" She was surprised. They hadn't exchanged numbers.

"I maintain a list of contacts for my entire team," he said casually, without looking up. "While we're collaborating on this project, that includes you and Mr. B." He slid the phone back into his pocket. "The contact list was part of the packet you received during our first meeting."

"Of course." Quinn tucked her hair behind her ear, embarrassed that she'd read more into the fact that Max had saved her number in his phone. "The list is in my portfolio."

"Good. See you tomorrow."

Quinn watched as Max trotted down the stairs. She locked up behind him and returned to the bedroom where they'd stood together moments ago.

She kicked off her shoes, stripped out of the gorgeous, pricey dress—a reminder of what almost was—and removed her makeup. She slipped on the white T-shirt that smelled faintly of Max. The soft, brushed cotton caressed her naked skin, abrading her already taut nipples and making her fully aware of the throbbing between her thighs.

Max hadn't kissed her, hadn't laid a hand on her there in the apartment. Yet, just being near him, her body ached for his touch.

Squeezing her thighs together, Quinn sucked in a deep breath and released it, trying to ignore the shiver that ran down her spine.

She slid beneath the covers, her body exhausted and ready for sleep. But her anxious mind won the battle. Quinn tossed and turned most of the night, inappropriate thoughts of Max filling her head.

Ten

Max stood by the bar in his parents' outdoor kitchen, quietly surveying the small crowd of friends and family. His mother was still over the moon about her anniversary gift and the prospect of establishing a new restaurant in the same space where her family's diner once stood.

"Mom hasn't been this giddy since Davis was born." Zora sipped her sweet tea.

"She was pretty happy when she learned that Savannah and Blake were pregnant again." Max nodded toward his sister-in-law, who stood on the other side of the space rubbing her protruding belly as she chatted happily with Quinn.

Quinn.

Aside from a cursory greeting when she'd first arrived, he'd tried his best to ignore her. But he couldn't seem to resist stealing glances at her.

She wore a basic, sleeveless minidress. But the cut of the dress gently hugged her full breasts, round bottom and curvy hips. The hem grazed her thighs and highlighted her toned muscles. And the deep turquoise color popped against her dark brown skin.

Her hair was twisted at the nape of her neck. Just a few strands hung loose near her temple, giving him an unobstructed view of her face. Quinn's broad smile was as bright as the midday sun. And something about the sound of her laughter filled his chest with a warmth that reminded him of those nights when she'd snuck to his loft over the barn to hang out with him.

"She's stunning, isn't she?" Zora commented quietly.

"Savannah?" He sipped his tea to cool the heat rising in his neck. "Yes, pregnancy definitely agrees with her."

"You know who I'm talking about." Zora could barely stifle a giggle. "The last time I saw that forlorn a look, it was when Cricket was staring at the pork chop in Davis's hand," she said, referring to Kayleigh's golden retriever.

Note to self: stop staring at Quinn like a lovesick fool.

Max finished his glass of tea and set it down on a nearby table with a thud.

"Actually, I was just keeping an eye on Savannah. She's probably uncomfortable out here in the heat. I'll take her a glass of tea."

He excused himself, retrieved two glasses of sweet tea from the beverage table, then made his way to Savannah and Quinn.

"I thought you ladies might like some refreshments," he said with a smile as he approached them.

"Yes!" Savannah proclaimed, fanning herself with one hand as she reached for the glass with the other. "Thanks, Max. You're a sweetheart." She took a long drink from the glass.

"How about you, Quinn?" Max held up the other glass.

"Sure. Thanks." She flashed an obligatory smile. That brought the total number of words she'd spoken to him so far today to four.

Savannah excused herself to go and check on Davis, who was playing with his cousin Benji's twins, Beau and Bailey. The kids got along well, but occasionally someone didn't want to share. Right now, that was Davis.

Max and Quinn stood in silence as she slowly sipped her tea and looked anywhere but at him.

"How was the apartment?" he asked. "Did you sleep well?"

"The apartment is perfect." She turned to face him. "Grandad is thrilled I won't be making that long drive back and forth every day. We're grateful to your family for providing it. That'll buy me time to find another place before Cole begins demolition."

Why was the mention of his brother's name like a bucket of ice water being poured over his head?

"I'm glad. And I'm sure we can help you find something else between now and then," he said.

"It was nice seeing Benji again." Quinn nodded toward his cousin and his fiancée, Sloane Sutton—the mother of their twins. "He has a beautiful family and he's done well for himself."

Benjamin was a tech genius who'd moved to Seattle, where he'd developed a healthcare tech app that he'd sold for more than two billion dollars a couple of years ago. And he and Sloane—Benji's older sister's best friend and his long-time crush—had hooked up at Blake and Savannah's wedding. Which had resulted in the twins and eventually their engagement.

Benji and Sloane's wedding was in a few weeks. After their honeymoon in Greece, their little family would spend a year in Japan while Benji oversaw a project for the company that had purchased his app. After that, they planned to settle down in Magnolia Lake where Cole was building a custom home for them.

"The marriage bug is hitting your family hard," Quinn teased. "Pretty soon, you and Cole will be the lone bachelors. Unless of course…"

"No, I'm not seeing anyone." He restrained a smile. "If that's what you're asking."

"I wasn't, at least not for the reason you're probably thinking," she said quickly.

He folded his arms, amused. "And just what do you think I'm thinking?"

She pressed a hand to her forehead and groaned. "God, this is awkward, isn't it?"

"It is." Max chuckled. "I was pretty shocked to see you come waltzing into the conference room that day, but the truth is it's good to see you again."

She sank her teeth into her lower lip and nodded. "It's good to see you again, too, Max."

He held her gaze, neither of them speaking. This time, the silence didn't feel uncomfortable.

"Zora," he said finally. "You forgot that Zora is still single, too."

"Is she, though?" They both turned toward where Zora sat on a sofa with Dallas, the two of them laughing. The corners of Quinn's mouth quirked in a soft smile. "I've been watching them for the past two days, and they behave like a couple if ever I've seen one."

Max studied his sister and her best friend. "I've mentioned as much to Zora before. She insists that what they have is a classic bromance. She just happens to be a girl."

"Cute explanation." Quinn laughed. "I'm not buying it, but it's cute just the same. Then again, dating must be tricky when you live in a small town *and* have four older brothers."

"Guess I hadn't really thought about that." Max rubbed the back of his neck as he watched Zora and Dallas. "But my sister is no pushover. She has never had a problem standing up to any of us. That includes my parents and my grandfather."

"I don't doubt that." Quinn smiled. "That doesn't mean she doesn't care what you all think. You're her family, and you're important to her. Of course, she wants your approval. The same goes for Cole."

"I doubt Cole much cares what any of us think." Max glanced over at his younger brother, who was playing with the kids. "Not everyone has that luxury. Some of us have obligations to fulfill."

He looked at Quinn and couldn't help the tinge of jealousy that arose at the sweet smile on her face as she watched Cole with the children.

"Children are an excellent judge of character, and they adore him," Quinn said. "He's a good uncle and a good friend." She turned back to Max. "In fact, he seems to get along well with everyone except you. And if you don't think that bothers him, you don't know your brother very well at all."

"Did Cole ask you to talk to me about—"

"Your dysfunctional relationship?" She laughed bitterly. "You must know Cole's much too proud for that. I doubt he's even willing to admit to himself how much it bothers him that nothing he does is right in your eyes."

"That isn't true." The accusation stabbed at Max's chest and heightened the guilt he already felt.

Yes, he was hard on his brother, but it was because he loved him and wanted the best for him.

"Cole is very good at what he does. Family or no, we wouldn't have engaged his services to renovate the barn or the restaurant if he wasn't the best man for the job," Max said. "And the house he built for our parents—" Max gestured toward it "—I honestly haven't seen finer craftsmanship anywhere."

"Maybe tell him that sometime." Quinn smiled softly, then sighed. "I'd better see if my grandfather needs anything. Thank you again for seeing me home last night."

He nodded. "Anytime, Quinn."

Max couldn't turn his gaze away from Quinn as she walked over to where their grandfathers were gathered with some of the other older folks in town. Sloane's grandfather, Atticus Ames, was among them. He bounced his great granddaughter on his knee, much to Bailey's delight.

Quinn was beautiful and no less opinionated than

she'd been that summer when they'd debated everything from sports to politics.

Now, as then, Quinn didn't pull any punches. She
had no qualms about calling him out on his bullshit,
a trait he admired in business and personal relationships.

Max thought he'd eradicated the feelings he'd
once had for Quinn. Instead, they'd clearly burrowed
deeper, lying in wait for the opportunity to reemerge.

Every moment he spent with Quinn rekindled those
feelings and stoked the fire he'd worked so hard to
extinguish.

He'd spent a single summer with Quinn Bazemore.
So why was it so damn hard to let go of their past?

Eleven

It was the beginning of a new week and Max found himself in another mandatory, impromptu meeting. This one had been called by his brother Parker—the company's chief financial officer. Max sat at the conference table with his father and grandfather, Parker, Blake and Zora, waiting for Parker to explain why he'd called this meeting when they were already inundated with work and exhausted from the previous weekend's festivities.

Parker pulled a stack of documents out of a manila folder and handed one to each of them.

Max read the title of the document aloud. "'Merit-based Succession vs. Birth-Order Succession in Family-Owned Businesses.' Parker, what the hell is this?"

Everyone else turned toward Parker, but Max glanced at Blake—next in line to become CEO of

King's Finest. There was no anger or confusion in Blake's expression. Only keen interest.

"Well, Parker?" Their grandfather frowned. "What exactly is this about?"

Parker pushed his glasses up the bridge of his nose. "If you'd turn to the introduction I've prepared on page one—"

"I don't want to read a prepared statement, son." Their father dropped the document onto the table with a thud without opening it. "If you're proposing what I think you're proposing, you'd damn well better have the balls to explain it yourself."

"All right." Parker set the document down.

He looked at their grandfather, then their father. Finally, his gaze settled on Blake with a hint of apology in his expression. It was a look they'd rarely seen from Parker before he'd started dating Kayleigh. His sister had teased that Kayleigh had sprinkled fairy dust on Parker and made him a real boy with real feelings.

That wasn't exactly true.

Parker had always been keenly aware of his own feelings, and still completely ruled by logic. Emotions didn't factor into his decisions. And he'd been a little too straightforward for his own good. Parker was still that person. His love for Kayleigh had simply shown him the power and usefulness of emotions like love and compassion. And he'd been making an effort to empathize with the people around him. So the pained look on Parker's face was alarming.

"Blake, you are a phenomenal operations manager. The efficiency with which you run the floor and the way you handle the staff… I'd venture that no one else at this table could handle either as well as you do," Parker said.

"Thanks, Park. That means quite a bit coming from you." Blake leaned back in his padded leather chair, his eyebrows lowering as he regarded his brother warily. "But?"

Everyone in the room turned back to Parker, as if they were watching a tennis match.

Parker cleared his throat and shoved his glasses up on his nose again. "You strictly adhere to company standards, and you ensure that your team does, too. It's one of the reasons King's Finest is known for producing some of the best bourbon on the market. But the soft center that makes you a great boss and an exemplary husband and father would be your Achilles' heel as the CEO."

"Seriously, Parker? That's what you're going with? Blake doesn't have an asshole mode, therefore he isn't tough enough to run the company?" Zora stared daggers at their brother.

"That's bullshit," Max said, taking up Blake's cause. "You just said yourself that no one else could run production the way Blake does. By your own logic, doesn't it follow that if he runs operations so well, he'll also run the entire company well?"

"Not necessarily." Parker shrugged, shoving his hands in his pockets. "How many great players in basketball or football turn out to be substandard coaches or GMs? You're not going to sit there and tell me that you think your all-time favorite basketball player is a good general manager, are you?"

"Point taken," Duke said gruffly. "But it's a hell

of a leap to say the same about your brother with no evidence to substantiate your claim."

"And that proof would come at what expense, Dad?" Parker asked. "Should we wait until the company is in decline before we declare that the experiment is a failure?"

Everyone at the table was outraged on Blake's behalf. Yet he just stared intently at Parker with an unreadable expression.

"You act as if King's Finest is struggling. We can afford to absorb a misstep or two," their grandfather said, then turned to Blake. "Not that I'm saying it would be a misstep to appoint you as CEO, son."

"It's okay, Gramps." Blake put a reassuring hand on their grandfather's shoulder.

"That's true," Parker acknowledged. "But we have the potential to achieve even more if we take a more aggressive approach."

"What's the upside of adopting a riskier approach when we're already seeing phenomenal results?" Zora demanded.

"That's the same thing we all thought initially when Savannah came to the company with her ideas about expanding our market share," Blake said quietly. "But she was right and the uptick in sales we've seen in the past three years is directly tied to the fact that we took a risk and adopted her suggestions."

"A project Blake encouraged us to take on," Max reminded Parker.

"True," Parker acknowledged. "But would Blake have had as favorable a view of Savannah's proposal if it hadn't been delivered by a beautiful woman to whom he was attracted?"

Blake stood abruptly and slammed his hand on the table. "If you want to question my leadership ability... fine. Do it. But don't bring my wife into this discussion. This has nothing to do with Savannah."

"That isn't a slight against Savannah." Parker held up a hand. "I hold her in the highest regard, as both my sister-in-law and as the event manager here. We're damn lucky to have Savannah as an employee and part owner of the company."

Parker inhaled deeply, then released a quiet sigh. "You don't have that killer instinct, Blake. Which makes you a great brother and a fine husband and father. But when it comes to our highly competitive industry, it's a fatal flaw."

"The liquor business has always been cutthroat, whether it was legal or not. Running moonshine was dangerous business back in my father's day," their grandfather said, referring to the company's namesake—his father, King Abbott. "And surely you don't think it was easy for me, as a black man, to enter into this business fifty-three years ago."

"Of course not, Grandad," Parker said. "Every single person at this table appreciates the sacrifices you made to start this company and establish a legacy for all of us. But we live in very different times. Everyone and their mother is starting a craft distillery these days. And some of the products are remarkably good. I'm not saying we need to regard the other companies out there as the enemy, but we have to take a focused, straightforward approach if we want to achieve our goal of being the best. That's the goal you established when you started this company fifty-three years ago.

I take that seriously. And I've proven my willingness to make hard sacrifices on behalf of the company."

"So now you're trying to leverage the fact that you were willing to play fake fiancée to Kayleigh in order to acquire her building?" Zora asked, her jaw dropping.

During the acrimonious negotiations to convince Kayleigh to sell her building, Parker had agreed to pose as her fiancé at the wedding of her ex's younger sister. Which had led to Parker becoming Kayleigh's actual fiancé.

"Really, Park?" Max laughed. "You're the one who came out ahead in that deal."

Everyone at the table chuckled.

"Definitely," Zora agreed. "Kayleigh is the best thing to ever happen to you, Parker. Plus, she took you on an all-expenses-paid trip to a tropical island. So don't try to spin this like you're some self-sacrificing martyr."

"She *is* the best thing that's ever happened to me, and I'm incredibly grateful to have her in my life," Parker admitted. "But I had no idea things would end up this way. I did something extremely uncomfortable for the greater good of the family and the future of this company."

"This is all a bunch of nonsense, Parker." Their father's face and cheeks were flushed, and his voice was strained. "I'm sorry that you somehow feel wronged because you weren't the firstborn, but that's just the way it is."

"That's not exactly true, either, son." Their grandfather chuckled, rubbing a hand over his thinning gray hair.

"What do you mean, Dad?" Duke asked.

"You were an only child." Joseph shrugged. "Not much competition there. You always knew that I was going to hand the company off to you. But what if you hadn't been an only child? What if you'd been second or third in line? Maybe you'd see Parker's argument differently."

The room grew quiet as they considered his grandfather's words.

They'd simply accepted that as firstborn, Blake was the one who'd be named CEO. Max had no doubt his brother would make a good CEO. But was he the *best* choice? It was a question he'd never considered. None of them had, except Parker, apparently.

"All right, Parker. Maybe you're right." Blake tapped the table, drawing everyone's attention. "This isn't some royal dynasty where birth order determines destiny. Nor do I want there to be any question about whether or not I deserved the position of CEO. I put a hell of a lot of thought into every hire I've ever made for this company. And I've never hired anyone—including Savannah—who I didn't feel was the absolute best candidate for the job. I care enough about Grandad's legacy to insist that the same care and effort be given to deciding who will one day replace Dad at the helm of this organization. So I agree that the decision should be merit based. And whatever choice Dad and Grandad make, I'll stand behind it."

The entire room fell silent. But no one seemed more surprised by Blake's concession than Parker.

"Now, if you'll excuse me, this marshmallow of a man has work to do." Blake stood, pushing his chair beneath the table and leaving the room.

They all sat in stunned silence, staring after him.

Did that mean Parker would be appointed the new company CEO? Max never had any qualms about working for Blake. But working for Parker? He wasn't sure who'd want to strangle his brother first—him or Zora.

Parker's mouth curved in a faint smile, as if he'd already achieved victory.

Zora folded her arms and stared Parker down. "If this is going to be a merit-based decision, that means the CEO–ship is open to any of us. That includes Max and me."

"Max lacks the killer instinct, same as Blake," Parker said flatly. "You have it in spades." He shook a finger in her direction, and she smiled proudly. "But while I struggle to figure emotion into the equation, it's nearly impossible for you to leave emotion out of any decision. With you, *everything* is personal."

"You're playing the emotion card because I'm a girl. How original," she said mockingly.

"No, I'm stating a fact because you're a hothead. The moment someone upsets you, you're ready to key their car." Parker stared at her.

He isn't wrong.

"I might think it, say it, dream about it. Maybe even threaten it. But I haven't keyed anyone's car to date," Zora argued.

They all stared at her and Duke raised an eyebrow.

"Okay, there was that one time. But that mofo totally deserved it."

The room erupted into laughter before it settled into an eerie quietness again.

"This is something your grandfather and I hadn't considered." Duke glanced over at their grandfather.

"So we'll need to discuss the matter ad nauseam." He stood, picking up the document Parker had prepared. "Don't expect a decision on this anytime soon." He pointed at Parker, then glanced around the room. "And no matter what, we're a family first. I hope all of you will keep that in mind. Greed and ambition have been the downfall of entire societies. They can easily destroy a family and a company like ours."

"Yes, sir," Max said. "We won't forget that. But if we are making the choice based on merit, Zora and I should be a part of the discussion, too. Regardless of what Parker thinks." He narrowed his gaze at his brother.

"Wouldn't have it any other way, son."

"I do have one question," Zora said to Parker. "This idea that you should be the CEO instead of Blake… Is Kayleigh behind it?"

They all regarded Parker carefully. He and Kayleigh were engaged now, but before then Kayleigh had hated their father, mistakenly believing he'd swindled her mother out of property once owned by her maternal grandfather.

She now knew the truth. Duke had been an anonymous benefactor to Kayleigh and her sister at the request of her now deceased mother. They'd embraced Kayleigh as part of their family. But maybe some residual animosity had prompted her to push Parker into making this power grab.

"No," Parker said adamantly. "This is something I've been thinking about for at least a year. I wanted to do my research first. Then I was looking for the right time to bring it up. Seemed like *after* the anniversary party would be wise."

Max stood. He'd heard all he needed to hear. He said goodbye to everyone and made his way back to his office.

"Ah…there you are, boss. The meeting didn't go too well, huh?" Molly's observation was more of a statement than a question. "Anyway, Quinn dropped by. She wants to know when you two can meet to go over some marketing ideas she has for your first event in two weeks."

Max grunted. Before, he'd been irritated that he had to relinquish control of his pet project to someone else. And now that he had just as much of a shot at becoming CEO as any of his siblings, he resented having to share the spotlight on a project that could sway the decision his way.

He rubbed the back of his neck. "Tell her I'm busy today. Maybe we can meet tomorrow afternoon."

Molly frowned. She knew his schedule better than he did, so she was well aware that he could spare Quinn an hour or two. But she didn't challenge him on it. She nodded, instead. "Will do. Can I get you anything?"

"No, thanks." He forced a smile and closed the door behind him.

His father had been clear that working with Quinn wasn't an option. But maybe he could change his mind.

Twelve

Quinn drove into town for lunch. Frustrated with Max's sudden lack of communication, she needed fresh air and a change of scenery.

She'd been working on the project furiously and had lots of exciting ideas to pitch to Max. But he'd been nearly impossible to reach all week.

Something is definitely going on with him.

Every time she'd tried to phone him her call rolled over to voice mail. When he was in the office, his door was closed. And Molly, who'd previously known her boss's schedule to the nanosecond, seemed utterly confused about when or if the man would ever have time to meet with her again.

Max was clearly avoiding her, and she intended to find out why.

As she entered the Magnolia Lake Bakery, Quinn

inhaled the aroma of the delicious peach tartlets they served. She'd definitely be having one or two of those.

"Quinn!" Savannah grinned. "Kayleigh and I were just leaving. I'm sorry we missed you."

"Me, too." Quinn said. "I would've enjoyed the company."

Quinn studied Savannah's warm smile, her brain churning. She needed help tackling the situation with Max, and she wasn't comfortable going to Duke, Grandpa Joe or her grandfather. It felt too much like tattling. But this deal was important to her family, and she wouldn't allow Max to sabotage it.

"Savannah, if you have a few minutes, I'd love to pick your brain about something," Quinn said.

"Of course." Savannah didn't hesitate. "Let's grab a seat. My back is killing me."

"And that's my cue to leave." Kayleigh smiled. "Besides, I have orders to fill and lots of packing to do."

Kayleigh hugged Savannah and bade them both goodbye before heading to her shop on the other side of Main Street.

"What's going on?" Savannah asked as soon as they'd settled into a booth near the window. "Have you run into a problem planning the marketing materials?"

Quinn explained her dilemma with Max.

"It's like he's become a totally different person in the past few days," Quinn said, wrapping up her concerns. "I'm not sure what I've done to tick the guy off."

"It isn't you, Quinn, so don't take it personally." Savannah's hazel eyes suddenly seemed sad. "There's a lot going on at KFD right now, and everyone is kind of on edge."

That tracked with what she'd noticed over the past few days. It wasn't just Max who seemed distracted. Zora and Blake seemed stressed. Duke and Grandpa Joe hadn't been around that much. Only Parker seemed unaffected by whatever was bothering the rest of the family.

"Max probably just needs time to sort through what's going on. You might actually miss the silence once things are back to normal," Savannah joked.

"Everything is okay with Duke and Grandpa Joe, I hope."

Savannah wasn't going into detail, and she respected that. After all, she had secrets of her own.

Everythang ain't for everybody to know.

Her grandmother's words rang out clear in her head.

"Yes, they're both fine," Savannah assured her.

"Good." Quinn was relieved. She genuinely liked both men. "And I get what you're saying about Max needing time. The problem is we haven't got much of it. Our first trade show is coming up soon."

Savannah frowned. "That is a problem."

She checked her watch, then climbed to her feet. "I have a meeting with a bride and her family at the barn, so I have to run. But I'd give Max until the end of the week. If he hasn't come around by then, do whatever it takes to snap him out of it. If you need reinforcements, I'm prepared to ride shotgun." Her warm smile returned.

Quinn thanked Savannah, hugging her as they parted ways. Then she ordered lunch, including a double order of peach tartlets.

She realized that Savannah's allegiance was to the

Abbotts. But Quinn liked her, and trusted that Savannah would keep her word.

So she'd take her advice and give Max a few more days to sort out whatever the hell was going on with his family. Then she'd put her foot down and do what she had to do to get this project back on track.

Because she needed to protect the interest of *her* family. And she wouldn't allow Max Abbott to get in the way of that.

Max was searching the file cabinet beside his desk for a document he needed when his cell phone rang.

Quinn.

He sighed, letting the call roll over to voice mail.

The three voice mails she'd left in the previous days made it clear she was beyond pissed.

Max wasn't exactly avoiding Quinn. He just didn't have anything new to report. Or rather, he didn't have anything he was ready to report to her since their last conversation. And since he'd been considering campaigns that went in a completely different direction from her idea, he needed to have everything in order before they spoke again.

It was after 5:00 p.m. on a Monday and it was turning out to be another long week.

There was a light tap on his closed office door.

"Come in, Molly," he called without looking up from the file cabinet.

The heavenly floral and citrus scent that wafted into his office indicated it wasn't Molly who'd entered.

Max turned around to see Quinn standing by his desk with one hand propped on a cocked hip and one eyebrow raised.

"Hello, Max." She folded her arms. "I realize that you're busy, but we need to talk."

"Hey, Quinn." Max cleared his throat and smoothed down his tie. "We do. I realize that. But now isn't the best time."

"Now is *never* the right time with you, Max." Quinn inched closer. "It's been over a week since we've had any traction on this project. Our first event is coming up soon, and there's a lot we still need to work out."

"Your concerns are valid, Quinn, and I promise to address them. But right now just isn't the best time."

"Look, Max, blowing me off in our personal lives, that's your prerogative. I accepted it and moved on. Blowing me off on this project is reckless and unprofessional." Her words came flying at him with increased speed and indignation. "This isn't about what happened between us. Or you being mad that Cole and I are friends. Our family legacies are at stake here, and I—"

"Good evening, Quinn." Zora stood up from the little table where she'd been sitting, blocked from Quinn's view.

"Oh, my God." Quinn's eyes widened. She pressed her fingertips to her mouth. "I didn't realize you two were in a meeting. I would never have... I'm sorry." She returned her attention to him. "Max, we can continue this discussion some other time."

"No, stay." Zora's tone was warm and understanding. She placed a gentle hand on Quinn's shoulder. "We were just chatting. Nothing urgent. It sounds like the two of you need to talk. It's been a long day, and

I'm ready to head home. Good night, Quinn. Good night, Max."

Zora gave Max a knowing glance, one that urged him to talk to Quinn. Something she'd been vocal about the past few days.

Don't shut her out, Max. Just tell her the truth. She'll understand.

Max clenched his hands in his lap as the door closed behind his sister.

There was a moment of heavy, awkward silence between them. Clearly, Quinn still hadn't recovered from the embarrassment of Zora having heard her entire rant. And he wasn't ready to say what he needed to say. But time was their enemy. He couldn't put off this conversation any longer.

Max shot to his feet and shoved one hand in his pocket. He gestured with the other for Quinn to take Zora's vacated seat and joined her at the table.

"I'm sorry." They both spoke at once, each seemingly surprised by the other's apology.

"I'm sorry I barged in on your meeting with Zora," Quinn said. "I would never have done that intentionally, and I certainly wouldn't have said the things I did about our past and about you and me and Cole. I assume she didn't know about any of it." Quinn tucked her hair behind her ear.

"Zora's part-time job is minding the business of everyone else in the family," Max said, only half-joking. "No, she didn't know, but she did suspect there was something between us."

"Which I just confirmed." Quinn groaned. "God, that was idiotic of me." She shook her head, then suddenly narrowed her gaze at him. "But I wouldn't have felt compelled to take such drastic action if you hadn't been acting like such a—"

"Ass?" He chuckled at her surprised reaction.

"I was going to say *child*." She folded her arms. "But I'll defer to your word choice because it's also accurate."

"I deserve that," Max admitted, dragging a hand down his face. "Which brings me to the fact that I'm sorry, too. I know it seems I've been avoiding you for the past few days…"

"And you're going to tell me you haven't been avoiding me?" She arched her eyebrow and crossed one leg over the other.

His attention was drawn to the smooth brown skin of her toned legs revealed below the fitted, knee-length black skirt. Max was sure his heart was suddenly beating faster.

"Okay, so I have been avoiding you," he admitted. "Mostly because my mood hasn't been conducive to conversation. Nothing against you personally."

"Mostly," she repeated the word. "So tell me about the part that does have to do with me personally."

He walked to the window overlooking King's Lake—the sole source of water for their world-renowned bourbon.

Quinn followed him to the window. "Everything seemed fine between us and then suddenly it wasn't."

He turned toward her. "Everything *is* fine between us. I've been contemplating whether it's the best use of resources for both of us to be working on the project."

Quinn's eyes widened and her mouth fell open. She clutched at her stomach, as if his words had caused her physical pain.

He hated being the cause of more pain for Quinn. But he hadn't created this situation; Parker had. He was simply trying his best to play the hand he'd been dealt.

"We've been through all of this," she reminded him. "My being here isn't a commentary on how competent you are at you job, and this isn't a competition."

He folded his arms over his chest as he studied her. *Damn, she's beautiful.*

His breathing became shallow as he tried to ignore her delicious scent and the electricity that rolled up his spine being this close to her.

He couldn't help remembering how good it had felt to hold her in his arms again on the dance floor at his parents' party.

"Maybe it isn't a competition for you, Quinn. But it is for me."

"I don't understand." She stepped closer, tipping her chin so their eyes met. "Who is it that you feel you're competing with? Certainly not me."

"No." He kneaded the knot at the back of his neck. Zora's words echoed in his ears. *Tell her the truth. She'll understand.* "I find myself in competition with my siblings."

"For?"

"Cone of silence?" he asked.

A slow smile spread across her lovely face, deepening the dimples he'd been obsessed with that summer. It'd given him a thrill to make her smile or to be the source of her unique laugh. "You're invoking *Get Smart* right now?" she asked. "Really?"

"Really, Agent 99." He leaned in closer, one side of his mouth curved in a smirk.

The familiar nickname prompted a giggle from her. The tension in his shoulders eased in response to the infectious sound, which invoked a kaleidoscope of fond memories. His chest ached with both deep want and gut-wrenching regret.

"Okay," she said begrudgingly, her wide brown eyes filled with curiosity. "Consider the cone of silence invoked." She gestured over her head, as if she was pulling a plastic dome down over it. "Now, tell me why you're being weird all of a sudden."

"Last week, Parker essentially declared that he should be the next KFD CEO." Max's shoulders tensed.

"Who did you expect to succeed your father as CEO? Blake?"

"Yes, because he's the oldest," Max confirmed. "But Parker believes the appointment should be merit based and that it should go to him."

"How did Blake take Parker's proposal?" Quinn asked.

"Better than Zora and I did," he admitted with a shrug.

"Neither of you anticipated being named as your father's successor, so why'd you take Parker's challenge so personally?"

Max ran a hand over his head and sighed. "Parker acts as if the only logical choice is between appointing Blake because he was born first or appointing Parker because he believes that he deserves it. As if Zora and I don't even warrant consideration."

Quinn nodded sympathetically. Her sincere expression was like warm water sluicing over the knotted muscles in his neck and back. A balm that soothed the anger and resentment the entire ordeal had stirred in him.

"I understand why that would be upsetting. After all, you're both an integral part of the organization," she said. "Did you tell Parker how that made you feel? Why you objected to him presenting the situation that way?"

Max turned to look at the placid waters of King's Lake. "We made it clear that if the decision is going to be merit based, it should be open to everyone. Grandad seemed to agree, and my father is considering it."

"That explains why the mood has been tense around here, but it doesn't explain why you seem upset with me."

"I'm not." He turned toward her again. "I'm sorry if I gave you that impression."

"Then why did you suddenly shut me out like I'm the enemy?" Her eyes searched his.

"If the decision is based on who has the biggest impact on the company..." His gaze dropped momentarily from hers and he shrugged. "I've been working on this project for a long time. Long before you got involved. And it's an excellent opportunity for me to demonstrate my value to our organization in an immediate, tangible way."

"You're dismissing me from the project? I thought you liked my proposal. Your entire family approved it."

The hurt in her voice brought back the day he'd called to end their relationship.

Why, Max? Was it something I did? Something I said?

The guilt of that day never seemed to leave him. It retreated to the recesses of his mind and heart, but it was never far-off. Always prepared to rear its ugly head again.

Today that guilt was front and center.

He was disappointing Quinn, again. And now, just as then, she was blaming herself when the culpability was all his.

"I do like your proposal." Max placed a gentle hand on her arm, drawing her gaze back to his again. "You're brilliant, Quinn. There's no doubt about that. Honestly, I've come up with dozens of different takes on this thing, and none of them have surpassed yours."

She sucked in a deep breath and her panicked expression transformed to one of pure bewilderment. "Then I don't understand. Why are you dismissing my proposal? Dismissing me?"

"I never planned to dismiss you from the project. I just hoped to come up with a better plan. A different direction that I would run point on." His thumb absently caressed her arm through the fabric of her sleeve. "It was a mistake, and I'm sorry for being such a jerk."

"Good." Quinn nodded. "Because if your goal is to impress your father and prove you're just as deserving of consideration, I can help you." She stepped closer and tugged on his tie, a teasing lilt in her voice. "I'm not your rival, Max. But I can be a damn good partner. If we work together, we'll impress both our families, and we'll each get what we want."

Her sweet scent filled his nostrils, and he could feel the heat radiating from her flawless brown skin. He couldn't help being mesmerized by this woman. If she asked him right now, he would've given her just about anything.

"Partners?" Quinn's eyes danced and her dimples were in full effect. She extended a hand.

"Partners." He shook her hand.

The sensation of her warm, soft skin against his stunned him, like an unexpected jolt of electricity. Max stood frozen as her eyes searched his.

Quinn slipped her hand from his and stepped backward. She turned toward the speaker mounted high on the wall. Music drifted down quietly from it.

She turned back to him. "'Make It Last Forever.'" A slow smile spread across her face. "Gosh, I remember every word of every song on that Keith Sweat album," she mused.

"I was definitely going through a Keith Sweat phase at the time." Max chuckled at the fond memories. "But c'mon, it's an R & B classic."

"True," she agreed. "And it would be more accurate to say you were going through an eighties and nineties R & B phase." Her eyes gleamed as she listed the artists he'd been obsessed with that summer. "Wow. That feels like forever ago. Come to think of it, you were supposed to make me a mixtape, which I never got."

He stared at her for a moment with his hands shoved in his pockets, debating his next move.

Would she consider him sweet and sentimental? Or would he come off as a pathetic sap?

Max rubbed his stubbled chin and sighed.

Fuck it.

He walked over to his desk, rummaged in the lap drawer and pulled out a plastic case. He handed it to her.

"You've got to be kidding me." She accepted the compact disc—a relic from their past.

"I made the CD, as promised." He sat on the front

edge of his desk. "I just never got the chance to give it to you."

"You kept it all this time?" She stood in front of him.

"I probably remember that summer more fondly than you do. But seeing you again after all this time threw me for a loop," he admitted. "I found the disc at my parents' place over the weekend in a box of my things from college. I couldn't bring myself to throw it out." He shrugged. "I brought it here to upload it to my computer."

Quinn stared at him, blinking. She seemed stunned.

"Why are you telling me this?" Her words came out in a rough whisper.

"I don't know." His heart beat rapidly. "I know you don't want to talk about our past." The sound of his own blood rushing filled his ears. "But it's all I've been thinking about lately. I messed up, Quinn. I hurt you, and I am so sorry for that."

"I should go." She turned to leave, but he caught her hand in his.

"I'm sorry if that upsets you. I thought you deserved to know that if I had the chance to go back and do things differently, I would. You have no idea how much I wish that were possible."

Quinn turned back to him, her eyes searching his before she put the jewel case down on his desk.

She was rejecting his gift. Rejecting him.

He should've kept his mouth shut.

"I appreciate your apology. Now, for the sake of this deal, I propose that we let go of the anger and guilt we both seem to feel about what happened that summer." She shrugged. "Maybe we could just hug it out and agree to move on. I hear that's what adults do."

Her sensual lips quirked in a half smile.

"I'd like that." Max grinned. Relief eased the tension in his chest. He opened his arms wide and she stepped forward, looping her arms around his neck as he hugged her waist.

Max allowed Quinn to dictate the physical interaction between them, grateful she'd at least given him the chance to apologize. She held onto him much longer than he'd expected.

Quinn had always given the best hugs. That hadn't changed. He welcomed the heat and the comfort of her embrace, unable to bring himself to be the first to pull away.

Finally, she dropped her arms from his neck. Rather than pulling away, Quinn cradled his face, caressing his stubbled cheek with her thumb as her gaze met his.

There was something so warm and comforting about her soft gaze. Without thought, Max grasped the hand that caressed his cheek and kissed her palm, then her wrist.

Quinn's hand trembled slightly, and she sank her teeth into her lower lip as she leaned in, eyes closed.

Max erased the sliver of space between them, tasting her full, sensual lips. Arms locked around her waist, he tugged her closer. His heart beat wildly in response to the sensation of her luscious curves crushed against his hard chest. He swallowed the sound of her soft sighs with his hungry kiss.

Since Quinn had come back into his life, he'd often found himself wondering what it would feel like to hold her in his arms and kiss her again.

His fantasies hadn't even come close to the reality.

He glided his hands down her back and over the full, round bottom, as firm and plump as the ripe, juicy summer peaches Bazemore Farms was so famous for. Max pulled her tighter against him, reveling in the sensation of her body pressed to his.

Quinn parted her lips on a sigh, and he slid his tongue between them, deepening their kiss. He savored the warm, sweet cinnamon taste of her velvety tongue. Her kiss was hotter and sweeter than he remembered. He honestly didn't think he'd ever get enough of it.

"You know, Max, I was thinking that... Oh, shit. Sorry." Zora had barged into his office unannounced.

Why hadn't he thought to lock that damn door?

Quinn slipped out of his arms and moved toward the window. With her back turned to them, she straightened her blouse and raked her fingers through her hair.

Max heaved a sigh as he glanced down at his lap. *Major hard-on situation.* Standing was not an option.

"What is it, Zora? I'm kind of busy."

"Obviously." She cast an amused glance in Quinn's direction.

"I thought you were leaving." He tried to keep the annoyance with his little sister out of his voice. After all, it wasn't unusual for them to pop into each other's offices. Though the circumstances were clearly different this time.

"I should go," Quinn said suddenly, hurrying past both of them toward the door. "Good night."

"Quinn!" he called after her. She didn't break her stride.

Max groaned, running a hand over his head.

"Sorry, I didn't realize you were entertaining company." Zora's expression was a mixture of contrition and amusement.

"How about knocking next time, Brat?" Max suggested. "And do me a favor—"

"I won't say anything to anyone. I promise," she interrupted. "I'll tell Quinn that myself, if you'd like."

"No, I should talk to her," he said, finally comfortable enough to stand. Nothing killed the mood like your little sister walking in on you. "What did you need?"

"It's nothing urgent. We'll talk tomorrow." She turned to leave. "Good night, Max."

He sighed, his eyes drifting closed at the soft click of the door behind his sister.

That went sideways fast.

Max honestly hadn't intended to kiss Quinn. He'd imagined it, ruminated over it and fantasized about it, without actually planning to do it. But once he held Quinn in his arms again, it was clear he'd never really gotten over her. That he wanted the chance to fix things between them.

Until Quinn had leaned in for a kiss, he hadn't believed that another chance with her was possible. After all, she'd insisted on behaving as if the intense summer they'd shared had never even happened. It had been driving him insane, because he could hardly think of anything else.

Max waited a beat and then followed the carpeted path to Quinn's desk. She wasn't there. She'd evidently fled the building, not just his office.

Hopefully, she hadn't encountered Zora on her way out.

Suddenly the ladies' room bathroom door opened, and Quinn appeared. Her brown eyes went wide, then she glanced around the space as if she expected another of his siblings to pop up.

"Zora's gone. For real this time," he said with a small smile, hoping to inject some humor into the situation and relieve the anxiety she was obviously feeling. "And I'm pretty sure everyone else is already gone. Parker and Blake don't stay late at the office much these days."

Her only response was a sigh of relief as she circumnavigated him and went to her desk. She pulled her purse out of the large bottom drawer and hitched it on her shoulder.

"I'd like to meet tomorrow morning to discuss the upcoming trade show." Her eyes didn't meet his. "If you can make the time."

"Of course, I can," he said, then leaned in closer and lowered his voice. "I realize how awkward that was in there." He jerked a thumb over his shoulder in the general direction of his office. "But you don't need to rush off."

She glared at him with fire in her eyes. As if that was the most ridiculous thing she'd ever heard.

Whatever progress he and Quinn had just made had been erased in an instant.

Thirteen

"**Y**ou shouldn't have followed me out here." Quinn scanned the space around them. Her heart was still racing. "Isn't it bad enough that your sister just walked in on us kissing?"

Technically, he'd kissed her. But she'd leaned in first. And the hug that precipitated the kiss had been her idea, too.

Quinn cringed. How could she have done something so stupid?

"We need to talk." Max's firm voice shook her from her panicked daze. "We can have the conversation here or in the privacy of my office," he added when she didn't respond.

Quinn huffed, then turned and followed Max back to his office. He closed the door behind them.

"This is a really bad look, Max." Quinn's cheeks flamed, and her pulse raced.

She'd lost it. She'd kissed Max right there in his office. And it hadn't felt like some random, isolated act. She'd felt like that starry-eyed girl falling for Max all over again. Which was crazy. Because she wasn't naive enough to fall for Max again. He'd shredded her heart to pieces once. Wasn't that enough?

Been there and done that. Spoiler alert: it does not end well.

Falling for Max Abbott again would only lead to another broken heart. And this time, she'd deserve it. Because experience had taught her better.

"No one is here except us," he assured her.

"It doesn't matter, Max." Quinn's head suddenly throbbed and her throat felt dry. "Zora saw us together." Quinn pressed a fist to her belly, her stomach in knots. "By the time we arrive here tomorrow morning, both of our families will know."

Her grandfather would be monumentally disappointed in her. Duke and Iris would never take her seriously again, and they certainly wouldn't refer her to any of their friends and business associates. And she could forget using her work here as a case study, which had been a critical piece of this for her.

Quinn squeezed her eyes shut and took slow, measured breaths. If only she could rewind the clock fifteen minutes. Before she'd gotten dreamy and nostalgic while listening to the unofficial soundtrack of that summer and remembering their first kiss. She opened her eyes and blinked back the tears she refused to let fall.

"I really screwed up." She shook her head.

"Zora won't say anything," Max assured her. "She promised me," he added, in response to her incredulous expression. "And she'd never give Parker that kind of ammunition against either of us. So you don't need to worry, Quinn. This isn't a big deal."

Quinn wished she could believe that. But even if Zora didn't tell anyone else, *she* knew. Even if she never mentioned it, the other woman would be judging her.

"Maybe your sister has walked in on you making out with a business associate before." She could barely contain the bitterness rising in her chest as the old wounds resurfaced. "But it's a first for me, and for me this could have very real consequences."

"What's that supposed to mean?" He frowned but didn't acknowledge her dig about him making out with other women in his office.

"It means my future is very much at stake here." Quinn smacked a hand to her chest. "I don't have the luxury of being an Abbott. For a moment, I allowed myself to forget that."

"I'd never stand by and let you take the fall for something I was clearly complicit in." Max sat on the edge of his desk again. "That goes for what happened just now and this entire project. Whatever happens, good or bad, we're partners in this. I'd never let you take the blame for me."

An eerie chill ran down Quinn's spine and she clenched her fists at her sides. She'd heard nearly the same promise before. The moment she'd chosen to believe it was the moment her career had begun to unravel.

She wouldn't fall for it again. *She* was the only person she could trust to safeguard her future.

"I kissed you, and I shouldn't have." Quinn didn't acknowledge his insistence that they were partners and that he'd protect her. "I lost my head momentarily. It won't happen again." She forced herself to meet his wounded gaze. "It *can't* happen again."

Deep wrinkles formed above Max's furrowed brows. He folded his arms and sighed. "If that's what you want, Quinn."

"It is." She tipped her chin, hoping she conveyed more conviction than she possessed at the moment. That her tone didn't betray her disappointment at how easily he'd acquiesced. As if she and the kiss really were no big deal for him. Already nearly forgotten.

"All right, Quinn. This is strictly a business relationship. Nothing more. And maybe, if I work really hard at it, I can pretend that summer never happened, too." His tone was biting.

Max had obviously been more perturbed by her refusal to discuss their past than she realized; nonetheless, it had been a good decision. Just look what had happened the moment she allowed herself the luxury of fondly revisiting their past.

Keeping their relationship strictly professional was in the best interest of her career and her heart—regardless of what her body wanted.

Because, even now, she wanted Max to kiss her again. She wanted to invite Max back to her place and get reacquainted with every inch of his body. To spend the rest of the night making love to him. She longed for the taste of his mouth, and her body ached for the pleasure of his touch.

She sucked in a deep breath, forced an uneasy smile and turned to leave.

"Wait." He held up the CD with *Mixtape for Peaches* scribbled on it in black permanent marker. "You forgot this."

A tiny piece of her heart crumbled, seeing those words and remembering the friendship and intimacy they'd once shared. A part of her wanted all those things with Max again, even knowing that revisiting the past would only lead to more disappointment.

"I appreciate the thought, Max. I really do. But maybe it's better if we leave the past in the past and focus on the future of this project. We both have a lot riding on it." She placed a gentle hand on his forearm and forced another smile, despite the electricity that filtered through her fingertips where her skin touched his. "I'll see you in the morning."

"Good night, Quinn." His voice sounded achingly sad.

She slipped out of his office, closing the door behind her.

It was better this way. Eventually, Max would realize it, too.

Quinn made her way to her car and took the narrow road toward town. She was angry with herself, and her eyes burned with tears. If anyone was aware of the consequences of mixing business and pleasure, it was her.

At the PR firm she'd worked for in Atlanta, she'd fallen for her boss's son. He'd pursued her for more than a year, and she'd finally given in. After a year of dating, he'd asked her to marry him.

She'd accepted Melvin Donaldson's proposal and

blown a mint on that Marchesa gown for their engagement party. But the week before the party, she'd walked into his office and discovered him seated at his desk, his pants unzipped and his secretary on her knees in front of him.

Quinn had dumped the lying, cheating bastard and tried to focus on doing the job she loved. Rather than being ashamed of his own behavior, he'd insisted she was making a big deal over nothing. That his encounter with his secretary hadn't meant that he didn't love her. He'd just been stressed and blowing off steam. And he'd been furious that she'd "humiliated" him by calling off their engagement after the party invites had already gone out.

Once it had become clear she wouldn't go back to Melvin, her corporate nightmare began. After being named Employee of the Year two of the previous three years, suddenly Melvin and his father, Oscar Donaldson—the head of the firm—found fault with everything she did. One by one, she'd been taken off the larger, more prestigious accounts. Worse, the Donaldsons had maligned her character to clients who'd complained about her being removed from their accounts. Finally, they'd manufactured cause to fire her. Her only recourse had been to quietly resign.

Embarrassed by the whole ordeal, Quinn hadn't told her grandfather the real reason she'd left the firm. Nor had she admitted the full extent of what had happened to Cole. Only her college roommate, Naomi, knew the truth. She'd called her friend in tears the day she'd been forced to resign.

Naomi had wanted her to hire a lawyer, and her friend was prepared to trash the firm online. She'd even suggested that Quinn talk to a reporter. Quinn decided she had suffered enough humiliation.

Even now, she hated herself for having been too much of a coward to stand up for herself. But she had no desire to become a poster girl for workplace romances gone wrong. And if she was being honest, she blamed herself for going against every instinct that had warned her not to get involved with Melvin.

She could still remember her father's words when she'd told her parents she was dating the boss's son.

Never crap where you eat, sweetheart. It won't end well.

Boy, had her father been right.

Quinn pulled into the parking lot of Kayleigh's building. She walked down the street to Margot's Pizzeria and ordered the personal-sized Hawaiian pizza Kayleigh and Parker had recommended so highly. Then she returned to the apartment with a piping-hot pizza in hand.

She'd agreed to let go of her anger over her and Max's past and just move on. And that still stood. But she wouldn't make the same mistake again. Especially not with a man who'd already let her down in the past.

Max had quickly agreed to her terms. So why had his easy and immediate acquiescence filled her with a deep sadness she couldn't quite explain?

It didn't matter. She just needed to get over herself and let go of the past. Her career and her grandfather's farm depended on it.

Max spent another hour working in his office with Vivaldi's *Four Seasons* playing softly in the background after Quinn left. He'd needed to switch from the mixtape of old-school R & B that he'd been playing incessantly for the past week. Nearly every one of those songs reminded him of cherished moments with Quinn that summer.

Maybe it's better if we leave the past in the past.

Quinn's words replayed in his head, like an old vinyl record with a deep scratch.

He'd quickly agreed to her request because Quinn was right. Neither of them could afford the distraction of trying to safely navigate the land mines of their past.

So why did a little voice in his head and the knot in his gut call BS on his agreement to let go of the past and move on?

What right did he have to be crushed by Quinn's refusal to explore what their kiss had meant? After all, he'd been the one who'd initially rebuffed her.

Quinn's rejection was a karmic dish of justice served cold.

Yet, he couldn't help the deep ache in his chest. How could Quinn walk away from a second chance for them so easily when he couldn't stop thinking of and wanting her?

He'd been young and stupid. Mostly, he'd been overwhelmed by the intensity of his feelings for Quinn. In her he saw his future set in stone: marriage, a home, kids.

All of the things neither of them had been ready for.

He wasn't the man Quinn deserved then. Maybe he still wasn't, but he wanted to be everything she deserved and more.

All of the things that had frightened him back then—thoughts of marriage and family—still seemed overwhelming. Yet, he found himself wondering if he and Quinn would have had all of those things together if he hadn't broken up with her.

Max dragged a hand down his face and sighed. He'd made his choice back then; now he had to live with it. Despite his growing feelings for Quinn, he'd respect her wishes and keep their relationship strictly professional.

He now regretted his decision to have Quinn accompany him to the trade show in San Francisco.

This trip would put his resolve to the ultimate test.

Fourteen

Quinn sat across from Zora in a booth at the Magnolia Lake Café. She politely waited for the other shoe to drop.

She'd made it all the way to Friday without anyone mentioning the kiss that Zora had walked in on. But when Zora insisted on treating Quinn to lunch today, she knew it was only a matter of time before Max's sister brought it up.

Instead, Zora had shown her photos her best friend, Dallas, had sent from his trip to Sweden. And she'd revealed some of their plans for the family-style restaurant they would be opening across the street.

When Quinn had finally started to relax, Zora pushed aside her empty plate and folded her hands on the table. "So about you and Max…"

Quinn nearly choked on a forkful of chicken pot-pie. She gulped down some water.

"Sorry, I didn't mean to startle you." Zora looked genuinely concerned. "I just wanted to say that I appreciate how awkward it must be for you and Max to work together. I don't know what happened between you two in the past, but you obviously have feelings for each other."

Quinn poked at the flaky crust and tender chunks of chicken with her fork. She shrugged. "It was a really long time ago, Zora."

"Didn't seem so long ago." Zora could barely contain her grin.

Touché.

"It's a mistake neither of us intends to repeat."

"Or maybe you two have been given a second chance at this."

"I didn't come here to reignite an old flame. I'm working with Max, despite our past. This is a golden opportunity to expand the reach of both of our families' companies."

"No one thinks you came here for Max," Zora assured her. "But if my interruption the other day derailed whatever might be going on with you two, I apologize. I like you, Quinn. And I can see why Max does, too."

"That's kind of you, Zora, and I appreciate it. But I'm sorry to disappoint you. There isn't anything happening between me and Max. That kiss was a one-off. We just got caught up in the moment."

"I respect that." Zora nodded. "But I also realize that a big family like ours can be a lot to deal with. Admittedly, a few of us are a little extra." She raised her hand slowly, and they both laughed, easing the tension. "So if your feelings for Max ever do change, know that I'm rooting for you two." Zora smiled. "Now, unless you decide otherwise, we'll never speak of this again." Zora locked her lips with an imaginary key, then tossed it over her shoulder.

Quinn grinned. Zora was extra, but she couldn't help liking Max's nosy little sister. She was well-meaning and obviously loved her brothers.

"Zora, Quinn." Benji approached the table holding his daughter, Bailey.

Quinn had gotten to know Benji and his fiancée, Sloane, a little at the anniversary party and brunch. They were a sweet couple with adorable one-year-old twins.

"Hi, Zora." Sloane, carrying their son Beau on her hip, leaned down and hugged the other woman. "Hi, Quinn." She surveyed their empty plates. "I wish we'd arrived earlier. We could've eaten together. That is, if you two don't mind eating with two ravenous toddlers who get more food on their bellies than in them." Sloane tickled her son's stomach and the boy doubled over with laughter.

"That would've been fun." Quinn jiggled Bailey's little foot, clad in a sparkly pink ballerina flat that complemented her pink tutu dress. The toddler giggled, burying her face in her father's shoulder.

"We were about to leave, but we can watch the twins while you get your order. And you can have our table." Zora glanced around the packed eatery.

"Thanks." Sloane handed Beau to Zora. The little boy was mesmerized by her dangling earrings.

Benji handed Bailey off to Quinn, and he and Sloane promised to return as quickly as possible.

"The twins are adorable." Quinn tickled Bailey, and the little girl laughed.

Spending time with the twins and Savannah and Blake's son, Davis, made her wish she had nieces and nephews of her own to spoil.

"And they're the sweetest children," Zora said wistfully as she tapped a finger on Beau's nose. "They make me want children of my own."

"The kids all adore you, and you're so patient with them," Quinn said. "You'd be an incredible mom."

"Now, I just need to find the right guy...or not," Zora said with a mischievous grin. "As my gram always used to say, there's more than one way to get a pickle in the jar."

Quinn burst out laughing as she bounced Bailey on her knee. "Wait, are you considering going to a sperm bank?" Quinn covered Bailey's ears and mouthed the last two words.

"Why not?" Zora shrugged. "I want kids now. What if the right guy doesn't come along for another ten years? Or what if I'm not able to have kids anymore when and if he does?"

"You've given this a lot of thought, haven't you?" Quinn moved the salt and pepper shakers beyond Bailey's reach.

"I've been thinking about it for at least six months." Zora kissed the top of Beau's head. "I honestly don't know why I just told you that. Please don't say anything. My family will freak out. I'm prepared to handle the flak, if I decide to go that route. But there's no point in riling them up when I'm still undecided."

"It's not my place to say anything." Quinn smiled reassuringly. "So this stays between us."

"Thank you." Zora seemed relieved. She jingled her car keys, then gave them to Beau so he'd let go of her earring.

Quinn admired Zora's clarity about what she wanted. Max's sister was outspoken and unapologetically direct, but Quinn liked her. And she'd grown increasingly fond of Max and his family.

She smoothed back the little girl's curls, bound by a frilly headband dotted with fabric flowers.

What would her little girl look like? Quinn couldn't help smiling but shook off the thought.

Zora's baby fever was contagious.

"You two are officially relieved of babysitting duty." Benji rolled up highchairs for the twins and helped load the kids in them. "And Quinn, Sloane dropped your invitation to our wedding in the mail yesterday."

"That's generous of you, but I don't want to throw off your seating arrangement." Quinn hated that they'd felt obligated to invite her.

"We want you there," Sloane insisted with a warm smile.

Quinn graciously accepted, then she and Zora said their goodbyes.

On the ride back to the office, they discussed Quinn and Max's upcoming trip to San Francisco. But like a silent movie playing in the background, her kiss with Max played on a loop in Quinn's head.

Maybe she couldn't get her brain to cooperate, but she had full control of her other body parts. This time there would be no reminiscing and she'd keep her hands and lips to herself.

Fifteen

Max sat up and leaned against the headboard, reaching for his cell phone on the nightstand in his darkened San Francisco hotel room. He checked the time and groaned.

Not quite six and he'd gotten very little sleep, despite turning in early.

He and Quinn had arrived the previous afternoon. They'd checked in at the trade show, set up the King's Finest booth, attended a mixer for sponsors, then enjoyed a lovely meal together at the premium steakhouse in the hotel.

Despite their rough start and the unexpected kiss, they'd managed to get back on track. Their collaboration had gone smoothly for the past week. They were finally working in sync toward a common goal, which also served their individual agendas.

With their unique creative styles and different approaches to problem solving, they complemented each other well. Max was proud of the campaign they were building.

By all accounts, he should've slept like a baby.

Instead, he'd been restless, tossing and turning the entire night. Not because he was nervous about the trade show. He simply couldn't stop thinking of Quinn. Wanting her.

She'd looked beautiful in a simple tan suit yesterday. The slim pants were tapered at the ankle, highlighting her strappy, nude-colored, high-heel sandals. The crisp white shirt she wore beneath it provided the perfect contrast to her gleaming brown skin.

He couldn't help wondering if Quinn's hair, worn in glossy beach waves combed to one side, was as smooth and silky as it appeared. And he couldn't stop remembering how luscious her full lips had felt when he'd kissed them or how firm her plump bottom had been when it filled his palms.

The thing that had kept him awake the most was the question that constantly churned in his brain.

What would've happened if Zora hadn't interrupted them?

The only topic that had gotten more rotation in his Quinn-preoccupied brain over the past weeks was how different their lives might be now if they'd stayed together back then.

He and Quinn had agreed to stick to business, and they'd both kept their word. They'd fallen into a relaxed rhythm and gotten comfortable enough with each other to talk about their families and fill each other in on their pasts. They discussed pop culture and current events. They'd even become comfortable enough with each other to joke around a bit.

The easy, familiar relationship they were building wasn't unlike the relationships he'd established with his assistant Molly and other members of his team. Yet, it clearly wasn't the same. No matter how much he tried to convince himself otherwise.

Max groaned and placed his feet on the floor.

No use staring at the ceiling for another hour.

He might as well do something constructive with his time.

Their first meeting today was with a buyer for a nationwide restaurant management company—JRS. They were meeting with the rep before the trade show opened. Getting up this early gave Max a couple of hours to swim—a great way to calm his nerves and get his head on straight.

When he got to the pool downstairs, he tugged his shirt over his head and tossed it onto a lounge chair with his towels and his phone before stepping beneath the poolside shower. But before he could get into the pool, his phone alerted him to a text message.

He picked up the phone.

Quinn.

He obviously wasn't the only one up early this morning.

Can we go over the presentation before we meet with JRS?

He typed in his response: At the pool. About to swim laps. Meet you at the buffet for breakfast at eight?

Three little dots appeared, signaling that she was typing her response: Eight is perfect. Meet you there.

Max slid his phone beneath his T-shirt, put on his waterproof audio player and turned on his old-school hip-hop playlist. He stepped off the deck, plunging into the cool water. Kicking off the tiled wall, he went directly into swimming laps.

Hopefully, an hour of swimming would silence the disquieting chatter in his head and prepare him to spend the next ten hours with Quinn—pretending he didn't want more than just a business relationship with her.

Quinn walked out of the coffee shop on the first floor of the hotel after ending her call with the rep from JRS. He'd rescheduled their appointment. She immediately dialed Max's cell.

No answer.

Not surprising, given that he'd texted her to say he was at the pool swimming laps. The phone rang several times, then rolled over to voice mail. Quinn was about to leave a message when a sign indicating the direction of the pool caught her eye.

She ended the call without leaving a message.

She'd once heard Parker say he didn't believe in coincidences. Maybe he was onto something.

If she left Max a voice mail, he might not get it for another hour. Someone else might have booked the JRS rep's remaining time slots by then. And if they missed their opportunity today, they might not get another.

It had sounded like the rep was hungover and too tired to make their early meeting. The man was evidently a partier. They needed to pin him down before he was either booked or too buzzed for a productive meeting.

JRS was the big fish she'd come here to bag. It was an account King's Finest Distillery didn't already have, and it would be a real coup for her and Max if they could get their new brandy and KFD's other products into the long list of JRS-managed restaurants.

Rather than heading toward the bank of elevators and returning to her room, Quinn followed the signs that directed her to the pool where Max was swimming laps.

She was going to the pool because it would be quicker if she simply strolled down there and nailed down a time with Max. It definitely wasn't because she was hoping to see him emerging from the pool half-dressed.

God, what if he's wearing a Speedo?

She would *never* be able to unsee that.

Quinn followed the signs to a bank of elevators that provided access to the pool and workout room. Hopefully, Max's text about going swimming hadn't been cryptic code for *I hooked up with some chick at the bar last night and I'm busy.*

A knot tightened in her stomach. It pained her to think of Max with someone else. But what right did she have to be jealous?

Quinn shook the thought from her head as she exited the elevator and made her way toward the wall of windows, cloudy with condensation.

She used her key card to enter the pool area. Only a few people were there. A hotel employee who was restocking towels greeted her warmly. There were two lap swimmers; one of them was Max.

Perfect.

Now she wouldn't have to traipse all over the hotel hunting him down in five-inch heels. She'd worn her open-toe Jimmy Choo platform sandals again today partly because they complemented her tan-and-black blazer and black knee-length skirt so well. Partly because Max hadn't been able to take his eyes off them yesterday.

Quinn stood motionless and watched him swim freestyle from her vantage point on the pool deck. She would've been content to sit there with a peachtini and watch him for hours. However, she needed to focus on her reason for coming here, and it wasn't to gawk at Max Abbott.

She walked over to the shallow end and waved to get his attention.

"Quinn?" Max didn't look happy about her intrusion as he tugged the red-and-black waterproof headphones from his ears.

He stood, rising above the shallow water that came up to his hips, and wiped the water from his eyes. Her gaze was drawn to the tattoos on his muscular chest.

Those were new. He hadn't had any ink on his brown skin that summer. She remembered their conversation about it like it was yesterday.

They'd been lying on an old blanket in the middle of a field, staring up at the stars that dotted the darkened sky.

She'd sat up suddenly and turned to him. "When I'm in a serious relationship and I *know* he's the one… I want to get matching tattoos. Maybe instead of rings." She'd only been half-joking.

At the time they'd kissed, had even made out a little, but they hadn't slept together or committed to each other in any way.

Max had chuckled, turned over on his side and traced a finger up her thigh, exposed by her tiny frayed jean shorts. "What tattoo would you get?"

Quinn had thought for a moment, then the perfect idea popped in her head. "I'd get a few lines from one of my favorite poems in a really pretty font."

"Wouldn't it be more significant if the poem was meaningful to the other person?" he'd asked.

She remembered so clearly how something about his answer had warmed her chest. In that moment, she'd truly believed Max Abbott was *the one*. That they'd forever be friends and eventually lovers.

She'd been wrong.

At eighteen, Quinn had been a dreamy teenager with a ridiculous crush while Max had been a man, three years her senior. Only a year away from joining his family's company.

"Quinn, what are you doing here?" Max's question brought her back to the present with all the ease of falling off a soft, dreamy cloud and crashing to the hard, dry earth.

Well, it's good to see you, too, Boo.

Max's chilly reception was a punch to the gut after she'd gotten lost in such a sweet memory. Quinn forced a smile, as if she was completely unfazed by his sour expression and brusque response.

"Martin, the JRS rep, canceled our scheduled

meeting this morning. I'm pretty sure he was hungover from last night."

"Okay?" Max folded his arms over his chest, accentuating his toned pecs and triceps. The move prompted her to peer more closely at the tattoo on the left side of his chest that he seemed to be intent on shielding from her.

"We need to reschedule the meeting, hopefully for later today. Marty gave us a few options. I wanted to see which time works best for you so I can get back to him as soon as possible, before someone else books our spot." She spoke quickly, the words tripping from her tongue so she could quickly let him return to his moment of peace. Still she couldn't take her eyes off the black ink etched into his brown skin.

Her eyes widened suddenly, and she sucked in a quiet breath. A chill ran the length of her spine. Quinn pressed her fingertips to her lips, her hand trembling.

She didn't consider herself vain or self-absorbed. And maybe she was making a self-aggrandizing assumption, but...

"Whatever time you pick is fine," he said gruffly. "Just tell me when and where."

"Let's take the one-o'clock spot. We can treat him to a pricey lunch before the show officially kicks off at three," she said absently. "Can I ask you something, Max?"

"Sure." There was apprehension in his voice, as if he anticipated her question. "Give me a sec."

Max climbed out of the pool, then asked the attendant for a couple of towels. He dried himself off before draping the towels over his shoulders. But she'd already seen the tattoos.

The letters QB were tattooed over his heart. Beneath that were a few lines of a poem she'd been obsessed with that summer: Robert Frost's "Stopping by Woods on a Snowy Evening."

The woods are lovely, dark and deep,
But I have promises to keep,
And miles to go before I sleep,
And miles to go before I sleep.

The lines of poetry were bordered by a rendering of woods in black ink.

"Is that…" She pointed at the tattoos. "Did you—"

"Yes." His voice was low.

There was only the sound of little splashes of water as the other swimmer continued his laps. Quinn stared up at Max, waiting for further explanation.

He offered none.

She pressed her fingers to her mouth, ruining her carefully applied lip gloss.

"How long have you had these?" she finally asked.

"Since a few months after we broke up."

Her gaze snapped up to his. She scowled.

"*We* didn't break up. You *dumped* me." She pointed at each of them in turn, underscoring her words. "With no real explanation, no discussion. So I'm having a really hard time understanding—"

"Maybe we should talk over there." Max turned and walked toward the lounge chairs at the far end of the pool.

Quinn followed him and stood with one hip cocked and her arms folded. "Why?" she asked impatiently. "Why would you have my initials and a quote from my favorite poem carved into your body *after* you dumped me? Who does that?" Her voice was unsteady and louder than she'd intended.

"I can only imagine all of the things that must be going through your head right now." He pulled on a white King's Finest T-shirt. "We can talk about this as much as you'd like but preferably not here." He glanced in the direction of the man in the pool and the attendant. Both seemed to be paying close attention to them now.

Quinn lowered her voice but ignored his request to take the conversation elsewhere. "I just need to know why you'd do this *after* it was over. In all these years, you never once tried to contact me."

"That isn't true." There was a pained expression on his face. He sighed and shook his head. "Not that it matters now."

"Of course, it matters. At least, it matters to me. So tell me… When was it that you reached out to me? Because I haven't received so much as a text message from you."

"That's because you changed your phone number." He folded his arms. "Couldn't have been more than a month afterward."

Quinn stood frozen, her heart beating harder.

She'd gotten a new phone a few weeks after Max had broken up with her. She'd decided to remove any temptation to call him and any anxiety about whether or not he'd call her. So she'd requested a new number and made a point of not transferring Max's contact info to her new phone.

But he would only know how quickly she'd changed her number if he'd tried to call her not long afterward.

"Our grandfathers have been best buddies since before either of us was born." She folded her arms defiantly, proud of her comeback. "If you'd really wanted to contact me, you would've found a way to do it."

"We managed to keep our relationship under the radar that summer," he said. "But how long do you think that would've lasted if I'd rung up your grandparents and asked for your new phone number?" Max raked his fingers through his damp hair and sighed. "You didn't want anyone to know about us, and I agreed. The last thing I was going to do was tip off your shotgun-toting grandfather that I'd spent the summer eating at his dinner table and secretly banging his granddaughter."

Now Quinn glanced around to see if anyone else could hear their conversation.

"You knew where I went to school. You could've written to me there."

"Do you *really* not know?" Max narrowed his gaze and stepped in closer.

"Do I really not know *what*? That my ex tagged his chest with my initials and favorite poem *after* he decided he wasn't that into me after all?"

"I *never* said I wasn't into you. If anything, I was too into you and it scared the shit out of me." He huffed. "I loved you, Quinn. But it felt like too much too soon. We were so young." Max rubbed the scruff on his chin. "I panicked and backed away. Within a month I realized I'd made a huge mistake. I tried to call you, but you'd changed your number. I couldn't go to your grandfather without breaking my promise to you. So I decided to go see you in person. I realized how royally I'd fucked up. I needed some grand gesture to prove to you how much I loved you and wanted you back."

He sighed heavily, as if reluctant to continue.

"I remembered what you said about the tattoos. That it was what you'd do once you were sure you'd found the person you wanted to be with for the rest of your life. So that's what I did. Then I hopped into my truck and drove all the way from my campus in Florida to yours in Virginia."

"Then why didn't I see you?" Quinn asked.

"I went to your dorm room and your roommate answered."

"My roommate?" She poked a thumb to her chest. "You must've gone to the wrong room. If you'd come to our dorm room, my roommate—"

"Nora… Natalie…" He frowned, trying to recall the name.

"Naomi." Quinn's heart plummeted to her stomach, then thumped so loudly that the sound filled her ears. Her chest felt heavy, like a tombstone lay on it.

The one she was going to erect after she murdered her college roommate.

"Naomi, right." Max snapped his fingers. "That was her name. Strawberry blonde with grayish blue eyes, about yay high." He leveled his hand just below the earphones hanging around his neck.

Quinn felt dizzy. Her head throbbed and her mouth was dry. "You met Naomi?"

"Fierce little thing." He chuckled bitterly. "Part pretty little coed, part pit bull, and a thousand percent protective of you."

Quinn couldn't have described Naomi better herself.

"She obviously knew exactly who I was and that you never wanted to see or hear from me again. Naomi hated my guts and she had no qualms about telling me *exactly* what she thought of me."

Max had definitely met her friend. She could only imagine how the encounter had gone. Quinn understood why Naomi would've hated Max. But why hadn't her friend told her that Max had driven up from Florida to see her?

"What did Naomi say?"

"I believe her exact words were, 'Fuck off, you fucking fucker, and leave my friend alone. She's finally happy again now and the last thing she needs is for you to pop 'round and fuck with her head, again.'" He said the words in a feigned British accent reminiscent of her friend's.

Naomi always did enjoy a good f-bomb.

"You'd gone to all the trouble of getting my initials tattooed on your skin and you let a five-foot-three-inch sprite run you off." Quinn folded her arms and tipped her chin defiantly.

"No." He sounded incredibly sad. "I told her I needed to hear it from you. That if you told me you didn't want to see me again, I'd walk away and never bother you again."

"And?"

He gathered his things from the lounge chair and shoved his cell phone into the pocket of his swim trunks. Then he turned to her and sighed.

"Naomi said you were out doing some other guy, and that she didn't expect that you'd be back anytime soon."

"And you believed her?"

Quinn hadn't dated anyone seriously for more than a year and a half after Max. But Quinn could easily imagine her roommate telling him such a lie to bruise his ego. Her overprotective friend would've tried to cut Max deep with her words after spending the previous two months nursing Quinn's broken heart and trying to cheer her up.

At the end of the two months, Quinn had promised herself and her friend that she wouldn't waste another moment of her life mooning over Max Abbott. That she never wanted to hear from or see Max again.

Naomi, evidently, hadn't trusted that Quinn would stick to her resolution when presented with the chance to see Max again. Instead, she'd made the decision for her. Quinn and Naomi had remained best friends, though Quinn had gotten a job in Atlanta and Naomi was now a married mother of two running her own kiddie clothing business in California. In all the years since college, her friend had never once revealed that Max had come to campus to see her.

"No, I didn't believe her." Max rubbed the back of his neck. "I hung around, parked outside of your dorm. If you didn't want to see me again, I would've respected that. But I wanted to hear it from you."

"So why didn't you ask me?"

"I saw the guy bring you home, and I saw him kiss you. I realized Naomi was right. You'd moved on, and you deserved better." Max's mouth twisted and deep wrinkles spanned his forehead.

Quinn thought back to that time in her life. She hadn't been seeing anyone. Maybe Max had mistaken someone else for her. She was about to tell him as much when she remembered the one guy who had kissed her around that time—Naomi's cousin, Rick. The guy her roommate had tried desperately to hook her up with. That explained why Naomi hadn't told her about Max's visit.

She didn't owe Max an explanation, but she had some choice words for her friend.

"Getting those tattoos before you knew if we'd get back together... That was—"

"Dumb?" he volunteered.

"I was going to say risky as hell," Quinn said. "You had no idea how I'd react or if I had, in fact, moved on."

"I realized what a gamble my grand gesture was." He patted his chest where her initials were carved into his skin. "That there was a good chance you still wouldn't forgive me. But I needed to show you how much you meant to me. And even if we never got back together, I guess I wanted to hold on to you in some small way." He rubbed at the tattoo through his shirt.

Quinn frowned, tears burning her eyes. She turned away from Max, abruptly changing the subject. "I should go make sure everything is ready."

"I'll walk you to the elevator." Max gestured toward the door.

Quinn nodded and went with him.

"How did you explain the tattoos to your friends and your family?" she asked after they had stepped into the elevator.

"I'd had them for a few years by the time anyone in my family saw them." Max punched each of their floor numbers. "I played the backup quarterback position for my school's football team. They assumed that was what the QB stood for, and I didn't correct them. As for the poem… Turns out I'm a fan of Robert Frost's poetry, too. More people have those words inked on them than you probably think."

"The way you ended things between us so abruptly without explanation… It seemed like what we'd shared never really meant anything to you. That I meant nothing to you. But—"

"You meant *everything* to me, Quinn." Max swallowed hard, his Adam's apple bobbing. "And it terrified me. I'm sorry I was a dick about it. I should've just been honest with you about how I was feeling, but—"

Quinn planted a hand on Max's chest, lifted onto her toes and pressed her lips to his—salty from the pool. She slipped her hands beneath the damp T-shirt and glided them up the strong muscles of his back.

Max backed her against the elevator wall, his tongue eagerly seeking hers. His hands glided down her body, gripping her bottom and hauling her against him. She could feel him hard against her belly.

The robotic voice alerted them that they were approaching their first stop—Max's floor.

He pulled his mouth from hers, both of them breathless as his dark gaze drank her in. Her mouth curved in a half smile.

She sank her teeth into her lower lip as she dragged her manicured nails over his skin. "Invite me to your room, Max," she breathed.

His eyes danced with excitement momentarily. Then he frowned and heaved a sigh.

"I think you know how much I'd like to take you up on your offer, Quinn." He twirled a strand of her hair around his finger, focusing on it rather than her eyes. "But I don't want you to regret this the way you regretted that kiss in my office. You were adamant about it never happening again."

Shit. She *had* said that, and at the time she'd meant it.

"That was before I knew the whole story." She pressed a palm to where her initials were inscribed on his skin.

The elevator jerked to a stop and the doors slid open, accompanied by the announcement of the floor number.

"I would *love* for you to come to my room, Quinn," he whispered, pressing a fleeting kiss to her lips. "But I never want to see the pain and disappointment in your eyes that I saw there after Zora interrupted us. I hurt you before. I won't do it again. So think about it. Make sure this is what you want. I'm in room 1709."

Max gave her another quick kiss and exited the elevator.

Quinn squeezed her eyes shut, her heart racing and her head still spinning from Max's kiss as the elevator continued its ascent to the twenty-fourth floor. She'd never been more confused about what she wanted than she was right now.

Her heart and body wanted to be with Max. But her brain reminded her that he'd let her down before and warned her that, if given the chance, he'd let her down again.

Sixteen

Max held the razor beneath the running water, then tapped the handle on the side of the sink before returning it to its carrying case. He preferred the look of a five-o'clock shadow, but he'd decided to shave this morning.

There was a knock at his hotel room door. *Good.* After his shower, he'd requested additional towels. He was barefoot and wearing only a pair of pants slung low on his hips. Max pulled on a short-sleeve shirt, quickly buttoned it and opened the door.

"You asked for fresh towels?" Quinn held up the stack of towels as if it was a silver platter. Her sensual mouth curved with an impish smirk that brought out her dimples. She broke into laughter. "Don't worry. I tipped the housekeeper. Is it okay if I come in?"

"Of course, thanks." He accepted the towels from

her and stepped aside to let her in, still a bit stunned she was there.

It'd been nearly an hour since he'd left Quinn in that elevator. As much as he'd hoped she'd come to his room, he'd assumed that she'd renewed her resolve not to get romantically involved. He'd even tried to convince himself that it was for the best. But now he hoped like hell that she'd changed her mind. Still, he wouldn't presume that was why she was here.

Max put the towels away. "What's up?"

"I contacted Marty. He's good with meeting us for lunch at one. He wants to go to the seafood place downstairs. You're not allergic, are you?"

"No." He gestured for her to have a seat in the living room. "The seafood restaurant at one is fine."

Quinn sat in the chair and he sat on the end of the couch nearest her. Neither of them spoke right away.

"It was nice of you to deliver the message," he said. "But you know you could've just called me or sent a text, right?"

Quinn nibbled on her lower lip, looking like a kid who'd gotten busted with a hand in the cookie jar. "I suppose that's true."

"So why'd you really come down here, Quinn?" He wanted to be clear about his intentions. And he needed her to be clear about hers, too.

Quinn set her purse on the small table beside the sofa and stood in front of him. She stripped off her jacket and dropped it on the chair she'd vacated. Her beaded nipples poked through the thin fabric of her camisole.

She slid her skirt up just enough to allow her to straddle him. Her knees dug into the sofa on either side of his hips.

"There is one other reason I wanted to see you." She captured his mouth with a soft, teasing kiss.

"I'm trying *really* hard to respect the boundaries you established, Quinn." His voice was a tortured whisper, which she seemed to relish. Like it fed the ravenous, seductive beast inside her. Something he remembered all too well. "You aren't making this very easy for me."

"Maybe I've changed my mind," she whispered between kisses to his jaw that sent blood rushing below his belt.

Quinn hadn't done anything like this since the summer she'd worn Max down, convincing him to give in to the attraction between them. Mostly because she'd won the battle yet lost the war. In the end, once she'd fallen for Max—heart and soul—he'd walked away.

Just as her mother had warned her.

Men only want fast girls for one reason. They have no intention of ever taking them home to their mothers.

Now here she was, the pull of Max Abbott so strong that she was ignoring her mother's advice again. She'd spent more than a decade being the "good girl." Being pursued rather than going after what she wanted. And what had it gotten her?

She'd ended up alone. Without a job. Her reputation tarnished.

This time she'd get what she wanted: sex with no strings attached. Then they could both just walk away.

"*Maybe* won't cut it, baby." Max held her chin between his finger and thumb, forcing her to meet his gaze. "You need to be sure."

Quinn's heart thudded in her chest as she grabbed her purse from the side table. She stuck a trembling hand inside and produced a small, overpriced box of condoms. "I went to the drugstore and got these." She waved them. "So yes, I'm sure."

Her cheeks and face flamed with heat. She'd never felt more vulnerable.

What if he says no?

The few seconds of silence that elapsed as he studied the box in her hand with furrowed brows were agonizing. Quinn swallowed hard, her pulse racing.

She was about to tell Max that she'd temporarily lost her mind, and he should disregard everything she'd said and done that morning. But then Max slid his arms around her and squeezed her bottom, pulling their bodies closer. His hardened length against her sensitive flesh sent a shiver of pleasure up her spine.

Max pressed his open mouth to hers, his tongue seeking hers in a kiss that was hungry and impatient. Heat spread throughout her body, emanating from every place he touched her—even through their clothing.

He tightened his embrace, his large hands on her back, crushing her breasts and sensitive nipples against his hard chest. She moved her hips, moaning into his mouth at the intense pleasure as she dragged her sensitive clit along the outline of his hardened shaft through the thin material of their clothes.

Max gently bit her lower lip before going in for a deeper kiss.

Her skin tingled, as if tiny licks of fire scampered across her flesh. Max Abbott was an excellent kisser. But now, just as then, he seemed hesitant to take things to the next level.

She'd come this far. *No turning back now.*

Quinn tugged up Max's shirt and skimmed her hands over the dusting of hair on his belly. As they continued the kiss, she slowly unbuttoned his shirt, starting from the bottom. Then she slid it from his shoulders, revealing the tattoos.

She broke their kiss, allowing herself the luxury of admiring the artwork. She traced the letters with her fingertip, applying only the lightest pressure.

QB. Her initials. Followed by her favorite lines from the poem she'd read to him that summer. Both tattoos had been there nearly the entire time they'd been apart.

Quinn pressed a soft kiss to those letters, brushing her lips over the words of poetry inked on his skin. Then she flicked his nipple with her tongue. He sucked in a deep breath, his muscles tensing.

Max speared his fingers into her hair, dragging her mouth to his again. Slipping his hands beneath the hem of the camisole, he tugged it over her head, then dropped it onto the floor. He fumbled with the clasp of her bra, releasing it and gliding it off her arms.

"Fuck," he muttered softly. His appreciative gaze trailed down her exposed torso, and her belly tightened in response.

She gasped in surprise when Max suddenly flipped her onto her back on the sofa and slid down her body. Taking one of the already ultra-sensitive nubs into his warm mouth, he grazed it with his teeth.

Quinn murmured softly in response to the sensation—part pleasure, part pain. She dug her fingers into his soft curls, gripping his hair as she arched her back in a greedy plea for more.

Max's mouth curved in a sensuous smile as his hooded gaze met hers. He shifted his attention to her other nipple, licking and teasing it with his tongue. Pleasure radiated throughout her body, her sex pulsing. Aching for his touch.

Gliding his hand down her side and beneath the short, black skirt, Max cupped the damp space between her thighs. He tugged aside the fabric, plunging a finger inside her as his thumb caressed the slick, hypersensitive bundle of nerves.

She trembled, unable to hold back quiet moans as he circled her clit with his thumb. Max slipped another finger inside her as he continued to lick and suck her sensitive nipple.

The symphony of varying sensations sent Quinn floating higher and higher, the intensity building until she'd reached a crescendo. She cried out in intense pleasure, her body shuddering and spent, yet craving more.

Her chest heaved with rapid, shallow breaths that left her slightly lightheaded.

Max trailed kisses up her chest and neck. Kissed the side of her face. Finally, he pressed a lingering kiss to her mouth. He stood, retrieving the box of condoms. His gaze held hers as he extended his open palm.

"Are you still with me, Quinn?"

Maybe this was a really terrible idea, but being

with Max felt amazing. And maybe she shouldn't, but she trusted Max to be discreet.

Standing on unsteady legs, Quinn nodded and placed her hand in his, following him to his bed.

Seventeen

Max hadn't yet mastered the fine art of resisting Quinn. Not when she'd been a smoking-hot college-bound freshman who had her sights set on him. Not now that she was a mature, incredibly beautiful woman who knew exactly what she wanted in the boardroom and was willing to go to the mat for it.

Then again, maybe his inability to resist her was because he wanted the same thing she wanted: to have her in his bed. Which was where she now lay.

He joined her in the bed and kissed her, relishing the sweet taste of her mouth and the feel of her soft lips. The glide of her tongue against his. Their kiss was feverish and hungry. Reminiscent of the desperate need they'd both felt that first time…so long ago.

Max was already on the edge, having watched her fall apart in his arms. He'd always loved the sweet little sounds she made, indicating that she was close or that she wanted more.

What was it about Quinn that had always made him feel a complete loss of control?

He glided his hands along the soft, smooth skin of her back. Inhaled her divine citrus scent and the smell of coconut wafting from her dark hair. Her quiet moans as they kissed ignited a raging fire inside him.

"You are so fucking sexy," he muttered against her lips. Max trailed kisses down her jaw, down her neck, through the valley between the glorious mounds of her full breasts, then down her belly. His gaze locked with hers. "I haven't stopped thinking about you since the day you waltzed this perfect ass into our conference room."

"Same." A wide smile lit Quinn's brown eyes as she slid her fingers into his hair. There was something so intimate about the gesture. "By the way, the look on your face that day—priceless."

"I'll bet." He pressed another kiss to her stomach as he glided the zipper down the side of the black skirt that had been tempting him all morning. Quinn lifted her hips, helping him slide the garment off. He took a moment to admire the gorgeous brown skin of her full hips and curvy thighs.

Quinn's belly rose and fell with shallow breaths as he laid kisses just above the waistband of her black panties. She gasped softly when he tugged the material down just enough to plant soft kisses on her hip bone.

The scent of her arousal teased him. Made his dick hard as steel. He was desperate to finally be inside her. Yet he wanted to savor every moment with her.

Max dragged the damp fabric down her hips and

off her legs. He spread her open with his thumbs and pressed a kiss to the glistening pink flesh between her thighs. He reveled in the salty sweet taste of her desire as his tongue traced the pink slit and lapped at the sensitive, swollen flesh.

Quinn shuddered. In a silent plea for more, she angled her hips, permitting him better access.

Max gladly obliged. He licked and teased her sex, then sucked on the distended bundle of nerves until she cried out. Her legs trembled and the space between her thighs pulsed.

He'd imagined this since the day she'd walked through the door of that conference room and set his world on fire, reminding him of all the things he'd tried so damn hard to forget. That he'd had the most amazing woman in his life, and he'd walked away from her because he'd been a coward. Terrified that one or both of them would regret committing to each other at such a young age. But the only thing he'd ever really regretted was letting Quinn go.

Max stripped off his remaining clothes and tore into the box of condoms, quickly ripping one from its foil packet and rolling it up his shaft. He teased her, pressing the head to her entrance before slowly pushing inside her warm, tight sheath.

He groaned at the searing pleasure of her flesh enveloping his, then slowly glided inside her until he was fully seated.

"God, Quinn, you feel so amazing," he growled, his voice so gruff he barely recognized it.

He leaned down and captured her open mouth in a kiss. Quinn dug her fingers into his back, her hips lifting to meet each stroke. He swallowed her soft mur-

murs as he moved inside her until she cried out with pleasure again. Until he followed her over the edge.

Max collapsed onto his back beside Quinn, both of them breathing heavily. An awkward silence descended over the room momentarily. When his breathing evened out again, Max rolled onto his side and planted a soft kiss on her lips. He sifted his fingers through her glossy strands of hair.

"No regrets?" It would kill him inside if Quinn regretted, even for a moment, what they'd just shared.

"None." A shy smile animated Quinn's dimples. She grazed the letters on his chest with her thumb and kissed him again.

Max discarded the condom, then crawled into bed. He cradled Quinn in his arms, with her bottom nestled against him, and kissed the shell of her ear. He'd be content to lie with this woman in his arms and not leave this room for the next three days. Until he'd convinced her that this time, things would be different. That he'd never hurt her again.

Max blinked, looking up at the brown-skinned goddess calling his name.

Quinn, who was fully dressed, shoved his shoulder again. "Max, you have to get up. We're scheduled to meet Marty in forty-five minutes and I still have to go to my room to shower and change." She put on an earring, which he vaguely remembered her losing at some point when they'd made love again.

"Wait…we're still planning on meeting the JRS guy for lunch?" He rubbed an eye as he propped himself up on his elbows. "I thought we were gonna spend a few more hours in bed." He tugged at the hem of her skirt.

She slapped his hand playfully. "There will be plenty of time for that later. Right now, I need to ensure that you're awake and that you'll be there on time. Remember, JRS is the white whale we came here for. Everything else is gravy."

"To be fair, he canceled on us first." Max dragged himself to a seated position, back pressed against the headboard.

"Max." Quinn used the same warning tone his mother had when he was a kid.

"Fine. But shouldn't we at least… I don't know." He rubbed the sleep from his eyes again. "Shouldn't we at least talk about what happened before you run off."

"It's a little late for a conversation about the birds and the bees." She dragged her fingers through her hair.

"I'm not talking about that and you know it."

"Then we're fine. I'm not a virgin this time."

"Which, to be fair, I had no idea about before the fact," he reminded her.

"I know." She smiled. "I'm just saying that while I have no regrets about what happened here, I also have no delusions that this is about anything more than sex for you…for us."

Wait…what?

Had he given her the impression that sex was all he wanted? Or was she making it clear that's all she wanted from him?

Either way, if that's the way you want to play this, sweetheart, fine.

"Good talk, Quinn."

"Look, this was fun, Max. No…" She shook her head, then gazed up dreamily. "This was…intense, and you were amazing. It took me back to that summer when everything between us felt so perfect. Everything was great until I tried to make it more than it was."

"And what was it, Quinn?" It was a sincere question. Because he knew what it had been for him: the best damn summer of his life—until he'd screwed up and lost the perfect girl.

"A summer fling. That's what it was then, and that's what this is now. Two old flames feeling a little nostalgic and reliving the past," she said. "But this time, we keep things simple and be honest with each other about where this is going. That way, no one gets caught up in their feelings or has any false expectations."

She leaned down and kissed him. "You still with me, Max?" She smirked.

Damn. She was using his line on him. But if this was the only way to keep Quinn in his life—in his bed—then he'd accept her terms. *For now.*

"Okay, Quinn." Max sighed. "What are the rules of engagement?"

Quinn sat on the edge of the bed and crossed her legs. She propped her chin on her fist, her foot bouncing, as she contemplated his question.

"The first rule of a secret summer fling is we don't talk about our secret summer fling—to anyone. Second, we only see each other on our business trips. Third, no overnights. We end the night in our own beds. Fourth, when we complete this project, we walk away. We both get closure and there are no hard feelings."

"Sounds like you've given this a lot of thought." He sifted a few strands of her hair through his fingers. "But things are never quite that simple. What happens if one of us doesn't want to walk away?" he asked.

She frowned, her nose crinkling. "We cross that bridge if we come to it," she said. "But there should be no expectations of anything beyond what I've outlined. Deal?"

"Deal," Max agreed. "But after the trade show today…"

She pressed a lingering kiss to his mouth and smiled. "Meet you back here then."

Max watched as she sashayed from his bedroom and into the main space where she retrieved her purse, then left his suite.

Heaving a sigh, Max got out of bed and hopped in the shower again.

He would play by Quinn's rules. But he looked forward to getting her to break each and every one of them. Because this time he had no intention of walking away so easily from the woman whose initials were branded on his skin.

Eighteen

Quinn sat cross-legged on the sofa in Kayleigh's rental apartment, exhausted after the conference in San Francisco. She hadn't realized how much walking was involved when attending a trade show. Then there were the early-morning meetings and the late nights spent in either her or Max's hotel room.

She and Max had spent nearly every waking hour together. When they weren't working, they'd shared meals, watched movies and spent lots of time discovering new ways to bring each other pleasure. All of it—except for a few meals—had taken place in private. The only thing they hadn't done together was sleep. At the end of the night, she either returned to her room or sent him, begrudgingly, back to his.

Quinn couldn't help smiling as she hugged her

knees to her chest. Her week with Max had been incredible.

They'd bagged the deal with JRS and gotten preorders from a slew of other clients, both current and new King's Finest buyers. The trip had been an all-around success.

So why was the time she'd spent with Max the thing she remembered most fondly? Quinn tried not to think too deeply about the reasons. *Why* didn't matter. Her stay in Magnolia Lake was temporary. She wasn't looking for a serious relationship and neither was he.

Her cell phone rang, and she couldn't help hoping it was Max.

She checked the caller ID.

Wrong brother.

"Hey, Cole. What's up?"

"Hey, Q. I know this is really, *really* last-minute…"

"I already don't like where this is going." She put Cole on speakerphone and went to the kitchen to make a snack. "Spit it out, Abbott. What do you need?"

She opened the fridge and took out fruit and cheese.

"I need you to be my plus-one, again," Cole said.

"For Benji and Sloane's wedding this weekend?"

"Yes. Say yes, *please*," he said. "I have three women dropping hints about being my date for this thing. I honestly just want to go, celebrate with my family and have fun."

Quinn put the fruit in a colander and rinsed it, then set it on the counter. "I'm surprised you want a date. I thought wedding receptions were a player's playground."

"I resent the term *player*. I'm up-front with every woman I've ever been with about not wanting anything serious. Plus, weddings might be great for hook-ups, but they also get women thinking about their own weddings. Like I said, I don't ever lead anyone on. So you'd be doing me a favor. We go as friends. I can enjoy the evening without anyone thinking that I'm going home with them or, worse, that I'd be their best bet for a wedding of their own."

"You're kind of a drama king. Anyone ever tell you that, Cole?" She sliced the apple.

"Only because I'm misunderstood." She could hear the grin in his voice. "Speaking of misunderstandings and drama… Us going to this thing together won't create any static between you and Max, right?"

The knife slipped and she cut herself. Blood oozed from her fingertip and dripped onto the cutting board.

"Shit."

There was a knot in the pit of her stomach.

The first rule of a secret summer fling is we don't talk about our secret summer fling—to anyone.

Had Max broken rule number one already? No, he wouldn't have talked to Cole about them. Had Zora broken her promise and told Cole about the kiss she'd seen? Or was Cole just fishing?

Relax.

"What's wrong?" Cole's voice was laced with concern.

"The knives here in Kayleigh's rental are surprisingly sharp. I sliced my finger." Quinn turned on the water and rinsed the cut beneath the faucet until the bleeding stopped. She cleared her throat. "Why would Max care about me going to Benji's wedding with you?"

Cole didn't respond right away.

"That was the vibe I got between you two at my parents' anniversary party," he said. "Max was... I guess the best word for it would be *territorial*."

Quinn breathed out a quiet sigh of relief.

They had agreed to keep things casual and not tell anyone. So going to Benji and Sloane's wedding with Max wasn't an option. No doubt, that was why he hadn't asked her to go with him, even though he knew Sloane had invited her.

Besides, Max knew that she and Cole were nothing more than friends.

"Max will be fine," she said. "The real dilemma is what am I going to wear?" Maybe Kayleigh had something in the shop downstairs that would work. "Never mind, I'll figure it out."

"So you'll come?" There was a lilt in Cole's voice whenever he convinced her to do something out of her comfort zone.

"I obviously have zero compunction about crashing your family's events, so why not?" She shrugged. "This time, I've actually been invited."

She glanced at the open but unanswered invite to Benji and Sloane's wedding on the counter.

"Awesome. That's the good news," he said. "The bad news is we're ahead of schedule on the restaurant project. Construction begins within the next two weeks. Which means—"

"Kayleigh and I both need to be out by then." Quinn sighed.

It looked like she'd be back to making that long daily commute again in a couple of weeks.

She made arrangements to meet Cole at the event on Saturday. He was in the wedding party, so even though she'd be his plus-one, she wouldn't see him until well into the reception.

Hanging out with Cole would be fun, and it would give her an excuse to see Max despite the rule she'd established about not seeing each other while they were in town. The truth was that she missed spending time with him. And she hated seeing Max around the office but pretending there was nothing between them.

Quinn picked up her phone again and typed a text message.

Hey, Max. Just an FYI. Cole asked me to be his plus-one at Sloane and Benji's wedding.

Three little dots showed up on the phone almost immediately. But after five minutes, there was still no message. Quinn put down the phone and went back to preparing her snack.

An hour later Max's single-word response came through.

Okay.

That was all he had to say?

But what exactly did she expect Max to say?

Don't go with my brother. Come with me instead.

Maybe he would've, if she hadn't insisted that they keep the relationship secret and not see each other in town.

You can't have it both ways, babe.

Quinn cursed to herself, grabbed her phone and wallet, and headed down to Kayleigh's shop.

* * *

Max watched as Benji and Sloane greeted some of their guests. He couldn't be happier for his cousin and his new bride.

Sloane was beautiful in a simple, strapless, ivory wedding gown. Her short pixie haircut was adorned with a crown made of fresh flowers.

Benji was a tech billionaire who could've easily afforded a huge, lavish destination wedding. But he and Sloane would've been content to get married by the justice of the peace.

Benji and Sloane considered the wedding to be the public formalization of what they already were: a family. The small, elegant ceremony and reception were simply concessions to their families. After their honeymoon, Benji, Sloane and the twins would spend a year in Japan. So it was the last time their entire extended family would be together until Parker and Kayleigh's wedding—scheduled for soon after Benji and Sloane's return.

Max had tried to stay in the moment, celebrating with his family. But he'd been distracted the instant Quinn walked in the door. She was stunning in a pale pink, backless dress with a beaded top. The ethereal, knee-length overlay made it seem as if Quinn floated around the room.

Still soaring after the incredible time they'd had together in San Francisco, Max was completely taken with her.

He could get accustomed to spending time with Quinn. She was brilliant at her job, and people loved her. She was affable yet persuasive. Fun to be around, and she had the best laugh. And though she was generally thoughtful and careful, there was a side of Quinn that was audacious and slightly uninhibited. He'd enjoyed every moment they'd spent together, and he was eager for their trip to Chicago in a few weeks.

But waiting three whole weeks to spend time with Quinn again didn't sit well with him. Being this close to her now only heightened his hunger for her.

Max had agreed to Quinn's terms, and he understood her hesitance to go public with their relationship while they worked together. But it didn't mean he had to like it.

As he watched Quinn dance with Cole, both of them laughing, he cursed himself for not sending his original text message. Or any of the ten messages he'd composed then deleted before finally sending his lame, one-word response.

Okay.

He definitely was *not* okay with Quinn being here with Cole. Max didn't care if the two of them were just friends. He wanted Quinn to be here with him. And only him.

Max had typed several variations of that message before finally deciding that coming off as jealous, possessive or downright needy would only scare her off.

He went with Option B instead: Just play it cool.

As if Quinn being here with his annoying younger brother was no big deal. Which now felt like the second dumbest idea he'd ever had. The decision his younger self had made to break up with Quinn definitely ranked first.

"Ask her to dance." Zora nudged his shoulder. "It's a wedding reception. There's nothing weird about that."

"Maybe." Max sipped his glass of bourbon neat.

Just the thought of holding Quinn in his arms again brought back vivid memories of their week together. Reminded him of how much he wanted her in his bed.

But sitting there watching Cole and Quinn together was another form of torture. He wasn't sure which was worse.

Max finished the last of his drink, then excused himself from the table before heading onto the dance floor.

He approached Cole and Quinn. "Mind if I cut in?"

"Only if you let me lead," Cole said.

Quinn broke out in her melodic laughter.

Max couldn't help laughing, too. "I meant I'd like to dance with Quinn, smart ass," he said before turning to her. "If you don't mind."

"Not at all." Her brown eyes danced.

Max took her hand and slipped an arm around her waist. They danced in silence for a few moments. "You look gorgeous, Quinn."

"Thank you." Her broad smile revealed the depth of her dimples. "You look pretty dashing in your tux."

He cradled her in his arms as they moved together, his hand pressed to the smooth, soft skin of her bare back. The sensation reminded him of how he'd skimmed his hands over her bare skin as she lay naked in his arms just a few days ago.

Max inhaled the familiar scent of coconut and citrus as he leaned in, whispering into her hair, "God, I've missed you."

She looked up at him. One corner of her mouth curved in an almost shy smile. "Me, too."

It was a small win. The first step toward making his case for breaking rule number two.

"I'm looking forward to Chicago," he said.

"For business or personal reasons?"

"Both," he admitted. "But I've been thinking—"

"Quinn, Benji had a brilliant idea," Cole appeared beside them suddenly with Benji in tow. "The cabin will be empty while he and Sloane are away."

"We'd rather have you stay there than for the place to sit empty," Benji explained.

It was a wonderful offer, though she doubted she could afford to rent the cabin of a tech billionaire.

"That's kind of you and Sloane, Benji. But I don't know if—"

"You'd be doing us a favor." Benji grinned. "You need a place to crash in town, and we could really use a house sitter while we're away." He shrugged. "I consider it a fair tradeoff."

Quinn agreed, thanking Benji for his generosity.

Max was glad Quinn would be staying in town once construction started on Kayleigh's building. But he hadn't finished his conversation with Quinn and couldn't help resenting his brother's awful timing.

Or maybe Cole had timed the situation perfectly.

Max assessed his younger brother coolly, but as usual, Cole was completely unfazed.

He forced a smile through clenched teeth, then put a discreet hand on Quinn's waist and leaned in to whisper in her ear. "Catch up with you later?"

Her brown eyes offered a quiet apology for the interruption. "Of course. Thank you for the dance."

Max nodded and walked away, heaving a quiet sigh. But if his past with Quinn had taught him anything it was not to give up so easily. He'd find another opportunity to make his proposal.

Quinn said goodbye to the bride and groom and to all of the Abbotts.

As she approached the valet stand, Max called her name.

"Leaving already?"

"It's been a long week," she said.

"True," Max agreed. "Mind if I walk you to your car instead?"

Quinn glanced over at the valet, who looked at them expectantly. She returned her gaze to Max. "It's a beautiful night. A short walk would be nice."

Max held out his hand and she gave him her ticket, which he used to retrieve her keys and get the location of her car. He extended his elbow to her and she slipped her arm through his.

It was a common, courteous gesture. But something about it felt warm and intimate, sending a small shiver up her spine.

"So we were talking about how much we enjoyed this past week together in San Francisco and how much we're looking forward to spending time together in Chicago," he repeated.

"All true," she agreed.

"But Chicago isn't for another three weeks, which feels like an eternity," Max said. "So I propose we nix rule number two. Because I'd *really* like to take you back to my place tonight, Quinn. We could spend the rest of this weekend in my bed."

"I'll admit that sounds intriguing, but this is a rather small town, Max." She glanced around the parking lot, suddenly conscious of whether anyone might overhear their conversation. "We agreed to be discreet about this. Hooking up here in town seems imprudent. Like we're asking to get caught."

Max stopped and turned to her. "Fortunately, my place is on the edge of town. Which is why it's the place my family is *least* likely to stop by unannounced. And once you move into the cabin… It's even farther out of town."

Quinn hiked an eyebrow.

"Seems you've given this idea quite a bit of thought."

"I've given *you* a lot of thought, Quinn." His voice was low and gruff as his dark eyes searched hers. "In fact, I haven't been able to think of much else."

His words, uttered so sincerely, filled her chest with warmth and short-circuited her brain.

But then, something about Max Abbott always had.

"It's already late tonight, but maybe I could come by your place sometime tomorrow."

One side of Max's mouth lifted in a crooked half smile. "I'll text you my address."

He saw her to her car. After the intimacy they'd shared over the past week, it seemed odd for him not to hug or kiss her goodnight. A part of her wanted him to—despite the risk.

Quinn released a quiet sigh as she drove away from Max, still standing there in the parking lot.

Do not fall for Max Abbott again.

But even as she repeated the warning in her head, it was clear that her heart had a mind of its own.

Nineteen

Quinn climbed back into Max's bed and cuddled against his broad chest. She traced her initials inscribed over his heart: something she often found herself doing absently as they lay together after making love.

They'd returned from the trade show in Chicago—another successful outing—and she'd moved into Benji and Sloane's cabin. But this Saturday evening, they were at Max's town house on the outskirts of Magnolia Lake. And he was unusually quiet.

Quinn lifted onto her elbow and stroked the whiskered chin that had sensitized her flesh as he'd kissed his way down her body earlier.

"There's obviously something on your mind tonight. Do you want to talk about it? Or would you prefer some space? If so, it's okay. I understand."

Max clamped a hand on her wrist. His dark eyes locked with hers. "What do you want, Quinn?"

Something about the question felt heavy and meaningful. He wasn't asking about her career. He was talking about them.

"You." The immediate, genuine response surprised her. Made her feel exposed. "*This*, I mean," she clarified.

"You've got me." He cradled her jaw, tracing her cheekbone with his thumb. "So now what do you want?"

"I don't know." She shrugged, keeping her tone light. "What do you want?"

"This isn't about me. This is about you being comfortable with asking for whatever you want." He pressed a lingering kiss to her lips. "Demanding whatever it is you need. You deserve that, Quinn. And any man worthy of you would be willing to give that to you."

"You're proposing we play a naughty game of Simon Says?"

He chuckled. "If it's easier to think of it that way."

Tempting. She swallowed hard, her skin on fire with the possibilities. A vision of this beautiful man on his knees worshipping her body flashed through her brain. "You're saying I should take control during sex? What brought this on?"

Max dragged a thumb across her lower lip. "Being with you is incredible, Quinn. But sometimes it feels like you're holding back. I don't want you to feel like you need to do that with me. You should say or do whatever feels good for you. Ask for whatever you need from me."

"Maybe you haven't noticed, but you do a pretty damn good job of anticipating what I want and what I need." She kissed him again. "I assure you—I have no complaints."

"I'm glad to hear it." Max trailed a finger along her collarbone, and she trembled slightly at his touch. "But I want this to be just as amazing for you as it is for me."

"In my experience, men don't take instructions in the bedroom very well. They consider it an attack on their manhood."

"Ah, you've been with one of those guys." He sighed. "The dumb, selfish fucks who never learn to please a woman because they're too concerned about getting off themselves. They don't realize how much better the experience would be if they'd learn to *thoroughly* please their partner."

Max brushed back her hair and tucked a few strands behind her ear. "If a dude gets upset because you're telling him what does or doesn't feel good to you, run. Because he's not just selfish in the bedroom. He's selfish about everything."

"God, that's true." Quinn sat up, scooting back against the headboard. She cleared her throat. "So all of the *skills* you've acquired… Never mind."

Quinn felt her cheeks getting warm as she smoothed the comforter over her lap. It was none of her business what Max had done in the years they'd been apart.

"Yes." He sat up beside her. "I learned by listening and observing, but also by asking." He stroked her cheek.

"What you've done and with whom…is none of my business."

Max's expression was suddenly serious. "Ask me anything you want to know, Quinn."

There was something so sincere in his gaze. Butterfly wings fluttered in her stomach. Her heart felt as if it might burst. She wasn't supposed to be falling for Max Abbott. She wasn't supposed to be feeling any of what she was feeling right now.

Quinn's breath hitched. "Make love to me, Max. Now."

Desire. That was the emotion she should focus on. Not whatever it was that made her feel like her heart might beat right out of her chest.

There was a momentary sadness in his expression. Her tactic wasn't lost on him. He'd wanted to do an emotional deep dive. She wanted sex, plain and simple.

"That's a command, not a question," he said.

"You said I should ask for whatever I want."

He chuckled, a grin spreading across his incredibly handsome face. "I did, didn't I?"

Max retrieved a strip of condoms from the nightstand and reached to turn off the bedside lamp.

"No." She stilled his hand, her heart racing as he met her gaze. "Leave the light on."

Max's eyes widened momentarily. Then a knowing grin curved the edges of his sensual mouth. "Yes, ma'am."

"And Max?" She trailed a hand down his stomach and cupped his growing erection.

"Yes?"

"How sturdy would you say this headboard is?" Quinn asked with a smile.

"Fuck," he whispered. "This is going to be one hell of a night, isn't it?"

It was, and she was going to enjoy every single minute of it. Because as good as things were between them, their little affair had a built-in expiration date. In a few months she'd leave Magnolia Lake, and eventually she'd return to Atlanta. But this time she'd walk away without expectations or regrets.

Max's eyes fluttered opened. An involuntary smile crept across his face. His night with Quinn had been beyond amazing. It was a reel that would replay in his head until the end of time. He reached for Quinn, but she was gone.

Rule number three: no overnights.

Max wasn't sure which he found more exasperating: being kicked out of Quinn's bed or waking to discover that she'd disappeared from his.

He grabbed his phone and checked the time. Apparently, great sex promoted sound sleep. He'd slept right through his alarm. Now he needed to hurry if he didn't want to be late for another Monday morning meeting.

Max climbed out of bed and headed for the shower, hoping the day would end better than it had started.

Twenty

"Nice of you to join us, son," Duke Abbott teased as Max slid into the leather chair beside Zora.

"Sorry, I…overslept." Were his cheeks as bright red as they felt? His sister's knowing grin provided a clear answer.

Max avoided Zora's gaze. "So what's this about?"

"Your grandfather and I have discussed Parker's proposal. We've decided that selecting the next CEO based on merit is a reasonable request," his father said.

"You're naming Parker as the next CEO?" Zora asked.

"We haven't decided who will be the next CEO." Duke gave Zora a pointed look. "We've simply decided the title will be earned, not inherited. I'm sure we can all agree that's fair."

Parker shoved his glasses up the bridge of his nose

and grinned. As if the crown had already been placed atop his peanut head.

"You can wipe that self-satisfied smirk off your face, Parker. You're not the only one who has a shot at this." The words left Max's mouth before he could rein them in. He was already cranky about waking up to a cold, empty bed after the night he and Quinn had shared. Now this. "So get over yourself and maybe take the self-righteousness down a notch."

"Maybe use that same energy you're coming at me with to step up your game," Parker suggested smugly.

Something in Max's head snapped. He jumped up and his chair tumbled backward, crashing to the floor. Max made his way toward Parker, who was sitting at the opposite end of the table from their father, like he was already king of the court.

Zora and his grandfather were calling Max's name, and Blake had rounded the table and stepped between him and Parker.

Blake braced his large hands on Max's shoulders. "Park is just trying to get a rise out of you, Max. No one here is questioning your abilities."

Max was still staring down Parker, who seemed oddly confused by the entire ordeal. As always, Parker said whatever popped into his head—the things most people mused about and didn't say aloud. It was difficult for him to know when to let thoughts just simmer in his brain rather than saying them.

Parker was making an admirable effort to do better in that regard when dealing with his fiancée. It would be nice if he tried a little harder where his family was concerned, too.

"Max, what's gotten into you, son? You've never

allowed your brother to get to you like this before," his father said.

When Max turned to respond, he noticed his grandfather clutching the back of his head.

"Gramps, are you okay?" Max asked.

"Suddenly got the worse headache of my life." The old man wavered, as if dizzy. "Think I've got a touch of..."

Grandpa Joseph slumped over onto the table, unable to finish his sentence.

Quinn had forgotten how therapeutic cooking could be. She'd loved spending time in the kitchen with her grandmother before a massive stroke had taken her from them.

She'd been cooking for three days straight in Benji and Sloane's state-of-the-art kitchen. A pot roast was going in the slow cooker. A ham was cooking in one of the ovens. A pot of collard greens cooked on the stove. And the surface of the granite countertop was dusted with flour and covered in strips of pie crust for the peach cobbler she was making.

Three days ago, she'd been floating around the office on a high after an amazing night with Max. Suddenly, an ambulance had come and taken Max's grandfather away. Everyone at the distillery was still stunned.

The indomitable Joseph Abbott had had a stroke caused by a blood clot, and he'd been hospitalized for the past three days, surrounded by his family.

She'd talked to Cole, who'd kept her updated on their grandfather's condition, and Zora, who'd mentioned that first day that they were eating God-awful food from the hospital cafeteria. Since then, Quinn had made it her mission to feed the Abbott family home-cooked meals, which Cole transported to the hospital. She'd probably cooked more in the past three days than she had in the past three years.

Quinn was grateful Joseph Abbott had chosen to work with Bazemore Farms, and she'd grown incredibly fond of the Abbott family. She was glad she could be there for them in some small way during such a stressful time. But more than anything, she wanted to be there for Max.

According to Zora, he blamed himself for his grandfather's stroke, despite the doctor's assurance that it was better that it happened at the office because they'd quickly gotten him medical assistance.

She'd tried calling Max, but he hadn't answered his phone. Nor had he responded to her text messages. He'd sent her a single email authorizing her to make any necessary decisions on his behalf regarding the brandy campaign—including representing King's Finest at the next trade show. And he'd copied his father, Zora and his assistant on it.

Quinn picked up her phone and reread the email for the fifth time. As if the terse business message might reveal something more. Like how Max was doing or if he needed her. Which was ridiculous.

She'd been the one who'd insisted on keeping their relationship a secret and on keeping it casual. What right did she have to be hurt by the fact that Max was clearly shutting her out now?

Quinn checked on the ham and greens, then typed out a text message to Zora.

How is Grandpa Joe?

Same.

How are all of you doing?

We're all holding up as best we can. Cole is trying to lighten everyone's spirits, but we're all on edge. Max is taking it especially hard. Still thinks this is his fault, though we've learned Gramps had a couple of mini strokes before this. Max hasn't slept much. Mom sent him home to get some sleep about an hour ago.

Give my love to Grandpa Joe and to everyone.

Will do. Thanks. We're all a wreck. You've been a godsend. Hugs

Quinn put down the phone, her heart breaking for Max. She could only imagine the guilt he was feeling. Max adored his grandfather. They all did. No wonder he'd taken it so hard.

Maybe Max wasn't ready to let her in or talk about what was bothering him. But hadn't she been the one who'd erected a wall around her heart first?

Max was simply following her lead.

She had laid out the rules. Rules meant to protect her heart and keep her from getting in too deep. But little by little she'd grown attached to Max and his family anyway. He'd been hinting at wanting more and trying to get her to open up to him. He'd even invited her to join him for Sunday night dinner at his parents' home—as a friend. But she'd maintained emotional distance, determined not to be hurt again.

Now it was Max who was keeping his distance. Reminding her of the casual nature of their relationship. They were business associates and fuck buddies. Not the person you turned to in a crisis.

It was what she thought she wanted. So why did she feel such a deep need to be there for Max? And so powerless because he wouldn't let her?

Maybe it was because the wound still felt so fresh from her own grandmother's death and her father's medical emergency just a few years ago. She'd allowed her emotions to cloud her judgment, let down her defenses and gotten involved in ill-advised relationships.

Was that what she was doing again?

Quinn washed her hands at the sink and returned to assembling the peach cobbler. She needed to focus on doing what she could to help the family. Especially since her own grandfather was in Arizona visiting his ill older brother. So she was making sure the Abbotts were well-fed and that their plans for the introduction of the new brandies continued to move forward.

It had been a long, somber day at the office, and she'd been cooking since she'd returned to the cabin. As soon as the ham and the cobbler were done, she'd turn in for the night.

Quinn preheated the second oven then hopped into the shower.

Afterward, she slipped on a short, vintage silk kimono she'd purchased at a little shop in Toronto a few years ago. There was something soothing about the brilliant turquoise hue and luxurious material with its colorful embroidery.

She returned to the kitchen to put the cobbler in the oven. Then she saw headlights approach, flashing through the front windows. She peeked outside.

Max.

He parked his SUV and got out.

Quinn's heart thudded in her chest. Had something happened since Zora's last text message?

She opened the front door, startling Max as he bounded up the stairs.

Lines creased his forehead and shadows hovered beneath dark eyes filled with sadness. He stepped inside, closing the door behind him.

"Max, is everything all—"

He captured her mouth in a hungry kiss that stole her breath and stoked the heat between her thighs.

She leaned into the kiss, parting her lips to give him access as his tongue sought hers. Lost in his kiss, everything faded away except his clean, woodsy scent and the warmth and solidity of his hard body.

Finally, Max pulled his mouth from hers, his chest heaving as he cradled her face in his large hands. His eyes met hers, as if there was something he needed to say, but he couldn't.

Oh no. No, no, no.

Quinn swallowed hard, panic filling her chest. She gripped the back of his T-shirt, terrified of the words Max couldn't bring himself to say.

"Baby, what is it? What's happened?" When he didn't answer, she prodded gently, "Tell me, Max. I'm here. Whatever you need, just—"

"*You*, Quinn," he said in a breathless whisper. "I need you."

He kissed her again, swallowing her gasp of surprise as he glided his hands down her body and lifted her.

Quinn hooked her legs around his waist. Gave into the comfort of his fiery kiss. Pushed aside the nagging questions about what his words meant beyond this moment.

He needed this. Needed her. And whether he was seeking solace in the arms of his lover or the luxury of losing himself to a few hours of passion, tonight she wanted to be that for him. To be a source of shelter from the storm brewing behind those dark eyes. Even if it was only for a little while.

Max carried her to bed. He toed off his shoes and stripped off his shirt, revealing the tattoos she'd kissed more times than she could remember.

The space between her thighs pulsed at the sight of this man's broad chest and toned body. His jeans hung low on his hips and her eyes were instantly drawn to the ridge beneath his zipper and then to the hungry gaze in his dark eyes as he climbed onto the bed, still wearing his jeans.

Max untied the sash of her silk robe. A wicked smile lit his dark eyes upon discovering she wore only panties beneath it. He pressed a sensuous kiss to her lips before trailing slow, tender kisses down her body. He seemed to relish each shudder of anticipation.

Hooking his thumbs in the waistband of her panties. he dragged them down her legs, dropping the scrap of fabric on the floor.

The hunger in his eyes made her belly flutter and something deep in her chest bloomed like a flower welcoming rays of sunlight. What she felt for Max wasn't just desire. It was need and something more.

Something she was afraid to give voice to—even in her own head.

When Max lapped at the sensitive nub between her thighs, all speculation about what tonight meant faded to the recesses of her mind. Her back arched and she clutched at the bedding as the sensation built with each stroke of his tongue.

He slid two fingers inside her, working them until her quiet whimpers ascended to desperate little pleas. Until body trembling, legs quivering and back arched, she tumbled over the edge, his name on her lips. Pleasure exploded in her center and radiated from her core, leaving her on a dreamy wave of indescribable bliss she'd only ever experienced with Max.

He crawled up the bed a little and laid his head on her stomach, his hand bracing her hip. Both of them were silent as she lay there with her eyes closed and her heart rate slowing. She placed a gentle hand on his head.

"Is it okay if I ask about Grandpa Joe now?"

Quinn wasn't being flippant or judgmental. She understood how Max must feel. She'd always appreciated inquiries about her father when he was ill, but there were times when she'd needed the mental reprieve of *not* discussing her father's health. Not being reminded that his life was teetering on the edge.

"Didn't leave much time for talk, did I?" Max's reserved chuckle vibrated against her skin. He kissed her belly. "The old man gave us quite a scare. But he got treatment quickly, and they expect him to make a complete recovery."

"It's okay to be overwhelmed by what happened, Max. I know how terrifying it is to almost lose someone you love." Quinn stroked his hair. "My dad suffered a heart attack a few years ago. He had to have triple bypass surgery. We'd just lost my grandmother a couple years earlier, so it was one of the scariest moments of my life."

Suddenly the timer blared in the other room.

"My peach cobbler." Quinn shot up. "Actually, it's *your* peach cobbler. I promised Zora I'd make one for your family, so I'd better not burn it."

Quinn slipped from beneath him and gave him a quick kiss before making a dash to the adjoining bathroom to freshen up.

"I won't be long." She slipped her robe back on. "But when I return, I don't expect to be the only one naked."

Max grinned. "Yes, ma'am."

Quinn hurried to the kitchen to get the cobbler out of the oven. It wasn't quite brown enough. But if she returned to a naked Max, there was a good chance she wouldn't make it out of the bedroom again. So she spent the extra ten minutes there in the kitchen jotting down her to-do list for the next day in her planner. And she tried not to overanalyze the words Max had uttered when he'd first arrived, the desperation in his eyes when he'd said them or the way they'd seemed to reach into her chest and squeeze her heart.

You, Quinn. I need you.

She shook the thought from her mind as she removed the ham and perfectly golden brown peach cobbler from the ovens and turned them off.

Quinn hurried back to the bedroom.

Max's jeans were on the floor, and he was in bed. His head was buried in the pillow as he snored softly.

She sighed, disappointed they wouldn't get to finish what they'd started.

Don't take it personally. The man has barely slept in three days.

Then there was the sheer mental exhaustion that accompanied anguish and guilt.

Quinn stood there frozen for a moment as she watched him. Max was an incredible man. A man she was definitely falling for. Or maybe she'd just never stopped loving him. Quinn pressed a soft kiss to Max's forehead and pulled the covers up over him. She stared at the empty space beside him.

Rule number three: no overnights.

It had been a hard rule. No exceptions. But wouldn't it be strange if she went to the guest room and left him alone here?

Quinn groaned quietly. Neither solution was perfect. But waking Max up and sending him home would just be plain cruel. Besides, if she was being honest, a part of her had always wondered what it would feel like to wake up with Max in her bed.

It seemed she would find out. Though this wasn't quite the scenario she'd imagined.

Twenty-One

Max woke the next morning, unsure of the time. He definitely wasn't at his own place. And though he was exhausted, he felt as if he'd been asleep for hours.

Rolling onto his back, he threw an arm across his forehead as he stared at the high ceilings with their exposed beams.

Benji and Sloane's cabin.

He glanced at the empty space beside him in bed, and the events of the previous night came rushing back. He'd crashed and burned spectacularly when Quinn had gone to the kitchen.

As desperately as he'd wanted to be with her, his body had won the battle. The sheer exhaustion of being at the hospital around the clock for the past three days had taken its toll, and he'd dozed off, breaking rule number three.

No overnights.

Unlike their decision to start seeing each other while in town, this wasn't something they'd discussed.

Not okay, Max.

He hadn't done it on purpose. But then again, maybe subconsciously he had. Because he'd wanted to spend the night with Quinn since that very first night at the hotel in San Francisco. And now things felt… different between them. Or maybe he was just projecting his own feelings onto Quinn.

Either way, he owed her an apology. First, for falling asleep before they'd actually gotten to the deed. Secondly, for staying over when it wasn't something she'd agreed to. And though he should probably just be content with their arrangement, a growing part of him needed to know where things stood between them. But first, he needed a shower. And he hoped to God there was a spare toothbrush around here somewhere.

After Max showered and got dressed, he followed the heavenly scent of bacon and waffles to the kitchen. Quinn was in that sexy little kimono again, but this time she wore a nightgown beneath it. Her hair was pulled into a messy topknot.

God, she was gorgeous. His mouth tugged into an involuntary grin.

How amazing would it be to wake up to this woman every morning?

Quinn gave him a sheepish smile, her brown eyes glinting in the sunlight. "Morning, sleepyhead."

"Sorry about that." Max dragged a hand down his face. "I don't sleep this late normally, and I know we don't do sleepovers…ever," he added.

Quinn flipped the bacon over on the griddle. "You

don't normally spend three days straight awake at the hospital, worrying about your grandfather's health, either. So there's that." She returned her attention to the stove, but there was tension in her voice.

Was Quinn minimizing his breaking of their no sleepover rule because she genuinely felt it wasn't a big deal? Or was it because it was a *huge* deal and she'd rather tiptoe around the subject than address what it might mean for both of them?

Max settled onto a bar stool. "I can't thank you enough for how you've taken care of my family. The food has been amazing and having home-cooked meals has been a source of comfort for us during all of this. I hadn't had your cooking since—"

"Since I helped my grandmother fix meals for the farmhands that summer." Her smile turned sad. "My repertoire has expanded considerably since then. Waffles?"

"Please." He pushed up his sleeves.

She handed him a mug of piping hot coffee and gestured toward the cream and sugar on the counter.

Quinn joined him at the kitchen island where they ate bacon and waffles with peach cobbler flavored syrup in near silence. Neither of them seemed eager to discuss last night.

"Thank you for breakfast. Everything was delicious." Max patted his stuffed belly and stood once they were done eating. "Let me get the dishes."

"I've got it." She stood, too, waving him off.

Max sank back onto his bar stool and cleared his throat. "About last night—"

"Last night was fine." She moved their dishes to

the sink. "Fantastic, in fact," she added with an almost shy smile. "I certainly have no complaints."

"Good to hear." He forced a small smile, uneasy about the wall she seemed to be erecting this morning. "Still, it was rude of me to fall asleep."

"Extenuating circumstances and all that."

Max walked over and slipped his arms around her waist. She smelled like summer peaches and sunshine and everything that was good about the summer they spent together. He nuzzled her neck.

Holding Quinn in his arms now didn't feel like revisiting the past. It felt like a glimpse into his future. But rather than dissolving into giggles or climbing him like a tree—her usual responses to him kissing the sensitive spot where her neck and shoulder met—Quinn's shoulders stiffened.

Max turned her in his arms and studied her face.

Was she angry with him?

"Look, Quinn, I know how this must seem... Me showing up at your door so late last night and then taking you straight to bed. But don't think that I—"

"If this is the part where you try to convince me that you didn't come here just for sex—don't. That's the very nature of our little arrangement." She smirked, returning to the dishes. "I'm obviously fine with that."

"True, but last night was about more than that—"

"You're under a lot of stress right now." She shrugged. "Sometimes, we just need the comfort of human connection to get us through those times."

She was minimizing what they'd shared last night. As if it was just a meaningless hookup.

It hadn't been.

And as hard as she was trying to convince herself otherwise, Quinn realized it, too. But then, being with Quinn had never felt inconsequential to Max. And despite the nature of their current arrangement, he doubted that any of their encounters had ever felt insignificant to her, either.

"Admittedly, once I saw you in this little robe," he teased, tugging at the silken material, "all bets were off. But I honestly didn't come here to take you to bed, Quinn. I came here because I really needed to see you." He lightly gripped her wrist to stop her from frantically scrubbing a pan.

The pan fell to the bottom of the sink with a clang.

"*Why* did you need to see me, Max?" She turned to him, nibbling on her lower lip. Despite asking the question, she seemed apprehensive about his answer.

His shoulders tensed and his heart beat double time.

Just tell her.

Max sucked in a deep breath, then slowly released it. "The past few days, I watched Blake and Parker at the hospital with Savannah and Kayleigh. They're both damn lucky to have them in their lives."

He hooked a finger in the sash of her robe and tugged her closer. She braced her hands on his chest to steady herself as she gazed up at him.

"Suddenly, I realized that all the things I've been feeling about us lately… I want that with you, Quinn. You're the only woman I've ever been able to imagine a future with. It scared the shit out of me that summer because neither of us was ready for it. But we're in a different place in our lives now. I'd like to see what the future has in store for us."

Quinn blinked; her lashes were wet. She seemed apprehensive. And the five or ten seconds of silence felt like an eternity to Max.

"That's incredibly sweet, Max." Quinn freed herself from his hold and swiped a finger beneath her teary eyes. "But this is a really emotional time for all of us and—"

"You think this is just some knee-jerk reaction to my grandfather's stroke?" Max asked.

"I'm not discounting your feelings," she said carefully. "But I can't risk mine on something that might only *seem* real to you now."

"If you're not interested in a relationship, I promise to respect that, Quinn. But if this is because—"

"I don't know if I can do this with you again." She blurted out the words suddenly, finally meeting his gaze for a moment before pacing the kitchen floor. "With a no-strings arrangement, there are no expectations, so no one gets hurt. But what you're proposing…that raises the stakes in a way I'm not sure either of us is prepared for."

Max rubbed absently at the ink on his chest. His wounded heart beat furiously beneath the long-healed skin.

Maybe she was right; he'd timed this poorly. But it didn't change how he felt.

Max placed his large hands on her shoulders to halt her frantic pacing. "You're telling me that this is really just about sex for you—nothing more?"

"I'm saying that I need to be sure of my feelings and yours," she said.

"I *am* sure of what I feel for you." He cupped her

cheek, his heart racing as she looked at him expectantly.

Say it. Now. Before you lose your nerve.

Max swallowed hard, his eyes not leaving hers. The
corners of his mouth curved in a soft smile.

"I'm in love with you, Quinn, and I don't want to
hide that anymore. I want to be with you and only
you because you are the most amazing woman, and I
am so damn proud of you. My heart belongs to you.
It always has. I want everyone to know I'm yours and
that you belong to me." He pressed a soft kiss to her
lips. "Is that clear enough?"

Her brown eyes were wide and glossy with tears.
She searched his face as if trying to determine the
answer to a question she had yet to ask.

Quinn stood frozen, her heart swelling with emotion and her eyes brimming with tears. There were
so many things she needed to say, but where did she
even begin?

"Talk to me, babe. Please." Max rubbed a hand
up and down her arm, as if trying to warm her. "Tell
me what's going on in that brilliant mind of yours."

Wringing her hands, Quinn walked over to the
front windows overlooking the lake. The sunlight fil-
tering through the window warmed her skin. She took
a deep breath, then sighed, turning back to face him.

"There's something I need to tell you. Something
I should've told you before now."

"Okay." Max kept his voice even, but worry lines
spanned his forehead. He extended a hand to her.
"Let's sit down and talk."

Quinn put her hand in his and he led her to the

sofa in the great room. He squeezed her hand, as if to encourage her, but waited patiently for her to speak.

She turned toward him and met his gaze.

"Last year, I was engaged to a man I worked with. He was my boss's son," she admitted quietly. "The engagement didn't last very long, but that beautiful Marchesa gown I wore to your parents' anniversary party...it was a splurge for what would've been my engagement party."

"What happened?" Max frowned, gently caressing the back of her hand with his thumb.

"I ended it when I discovered him with his secretary. He felt I was overreacting. His father, who owned the firm, agreed. Neither of them took my rejection well. I stayed on, tried to be professional, like none of it had ever happened. But they held a grudge and eventually pushed me out of the firm. Due to a noncompete clause, I had to wait at least a year before I could work in the industry there again. That's the real reason I left Atlanta."

Quinn's cheeks stung and a knot tightened in her gut from the sheer humiliation of reliving that entire ordeal. One she should've seen coming.

She wiped angrily at the hot tears that leaked from the corners of her eyes. "Just like that, I flushed my career down the drain."

"I'm sorry you had to endure that, Quinn. But you're not to blame for what happened."

"Aren't I?" She tugged her hand from his and smoothed loose strands of hair before securing the knot atop her head. "I should never have gotten involved with my boss's son, and now I..." She sighed, letting her words trail off.

"And now you're afraid you're making the same mistake by getting involved with me." Max rubbed his chin. "So it's not just our history I'm battling. It's your history with him, too."

She shifted her gaze from his without response.

"Quinn, look at me." Max took her hand in his again, meeting her gaze. "I know I hurt you, and I am *really* sorry. I was young and stupid, and I had a lot to learn. I don't blame you for being wary about getting involved with me again. But sweetheart, I'm *not that* guy you were engaged to. I'm not even the guy I was thirteen years ago. Hurting you is the single biggest regret of my life, Quinn. We've been given another chance at our happy ending. There's no way I'm going to screw this up again. I promise you that."

She wanted to believe she could trust Max and that he wouldn't hurt her again. Because she wanted to be with him, too. She'd mused over the idea. Fantasized about what a real, adult relationship between them would be like. But the cautious part of her that had erected a fort around her heart to protect it was still terrified of taking the leap.

Once bitten, twice shy.

"I know you want an answer right now, Max, but—"

"No pressure, beautiful. I understand now. Take whatever time you need." Max stood, giving her a half smile. "Thank you again for breakfast. I'd better get back to the hospital."

"Thank you for last night." Quinn flashed a playful grin, hoping it masked the uneasiness she felt. She lifted onto her toes and pressed a tame kiss to his lips.

Max cradled her face and deepened their kiss, filling her body with heat and making her wish they could pick up where they'd left off last night.

Suddenly, he broke the kiss and released her.

Quinn's body protested. Her nipples throbbed and there was an insistent pulse between her thighs.

He lifted her chin gently, so their eyes met. "I'm sorry for what you went through in Atlanta, Quinn, and I'm glad you felt comfortable enough to share that with me. But that asshole's loss is our gain. I'm grateful you've come back into my life. These past few months have been so special for me, Quinn. I hope they have been for you, too."

Max pulled away, not waiting for a response. He shifted the topic instead. "You mentioned a care package you wanted me to take back to the hospital."

"Yes, right." She pulled the cardboard box neatly packed with all of the food she'd prepared out of the stainless steel refrigerator. Then she watched as Max loaded up his SUV and drove away. She sighed, missing him already.

Quinn checked her phone. She had a conference call soon with one of the vendors they'd met in Chicago.

Her personal life was a complicated mess, but at least the joint brandy project—though still in its infancy—had already hit a homerun. They'd inked a deal with JRS to carry the KFD line, including their brandies, in all of the restaurants they managed nationwide.

After tasting the product, vendors were clamoring for it and preorders already far exceeded even their most ambitious projections. Duke had indicated that they needed to discuss the possibility of expanding the facilities so they could increase production.

In a few more months, she would turn the project over to Max to be handled in-house, so she could go back to concentrating on the farm and on developing her own consultancy. News that should've thrilled her. But the thought of walking away from Max made her chest ache.

This was supposed to be purely physical and just for fun. No hearts involved.

So much for her simple plan.

She hadn't expected Max would spend the night. She certainly hadn't anticipated that he'd declare that he loved her and wanted a future with her. But Quinn had lain awake after nights with Max wondering if things could work out between them this time or if she was just setting herself up for more heartbreak. She'd had more than enough of that.

Fear is a piss-poor decision-maker. Don't ever make a decision strictly out of fear.

More of her grandmother's wisdom, which she'd invariably heeded in her career. But was she brave enough to follow her advice when it came to her heart?

Twenty-Two

Quinn paid the cashier for two caramel vanilla lattes and found an empty table in a secluded area of the hospital cafeteria. She slid into the chair and wrapped her hands around one of the steaming hot paper cups. A group of women in white jackets and colorful scrubs sat a couple of tables away.

Work had kept her preoccupied for the past two days. But not busy enough to prevent her from obsessively reflecting on her conversation with Max at the cabin. In quiet moments, his words echoed in her head. She could recall nearly every word, every gesture, every expression he'd used. She remembered that he'd smelled of her soap. His mouth had tasted like rich caramel-pecan bourbon coffee and there was a hint of the peach cobbler syrup she'd brought from Georgia by the case on his sensuous lips.

I'm in love with you, Quinn.

I want to be with you and only you.

I want everyone to know I'm yours and that you belong to me.

Those phrases had replayed in her head again and again for the past two days as she'd sorted through her jumble of emotions, confronted her immobilizing fears, and contemplated the realities of a future with Max Abbott—the man she'd first fallen in love with in that misty haze of being a wide-eyed college freshman.

"Quinn, hey." Max looked handsome but tired as he approached the table. He wore a button-down shirt and a pair of broken-in jeans.

"How's Grandpa Joe doing?" She resisted the urge to bound out of the chair and wrap her arms and legs around him. It'd only been two days since she'd seen him. Yet she'd missed him desperately, and she had been counting the hours until she would see him again.

"Gramps is good, all things considered. Full of fire and ready to blow this joint. He'll probably outlive us all." Max seemed to debate whether he should hug her. But he sat down in the chair opposite her and folded his hands on the table instead. "Thanks for meeting me here. They're running a battery of tests on Gramps, and I wanted to be here for them."

"I thought maybe you could use some coffee." She slid the paper cup toward him.

"Thanks." He gripped it but didn't take a sip. His attention was focused on her. "You wanted to talk?"

"I do." Quinn widened her nervous smile and

tucked her hair behind one ear. She extended her hands across the table, palms open.

Max relaxed his cautious smile. His dark eyes seemed hopeful as he took her hands.

After all of the nights they'd spent together over the past few months, his touch still made her skin tingle and sent chills up and down her spine.

"The other day, when you said that…" Quinn stumbled over the word. She'd repeated Max's declaration in her head again and again, but this was the first time she was saying the words aloud.

"That I'm in love with you?" he offered, a smirk curving one side of his mouth. He was barely able to contain his amusement and seemed to get a kick out of being the one on the offensive this time around.

"Yes." She took a deep breath before meeting his gaze again. "It was a really beautiful moment. But when you compared what you wanted with me to what Blake and Savannah have… I'll admit it freaked me out a little."

"It kind of freaked me out to realize it." He brushed his lips over the back of her hand. "But it's the truth. We've already missed so much time together, Quinn, and I know that's my fault," he added quickly. "But I don't want to miss another minute with you. I want you in my life, in my bed. I want you to be my plus-one. And I want you beside me at those Sunday night family dinners. To quote Roger Troutman, I want to be your man. Plain and simple."

Quinn laughed at his mention of yet another song he'd played for her that summer. Her vision blurred with tears. "Good. Because I love you, too, Max. And I want all of those things with you, too."

"God, I'm glad to hear you say that." He stood, rounding the table and pulling her into a tight hug. Max breathed a sigh of relief that gently rustled her hair. "When I didn't hear anything from you the past couple of days... I'll admit I was a little worried." He chuckled. "But I would've waited for as long as it took to hear those words." He gave her a quick kiss, his gaze lingering on her lips.

"We should get out of here before we're thrown out for making out in the hospital cafeteria." Quinn's cheeks warmed as she glanced around at the people staring at them.

"Good idea. Besides, Gramps is really looking forward to seeing you," Max said. "Walk back with me?"

She nodded and they grabbed their lukewarm coffees and linked hands as he led her toward a bank of elevators. Max pushed the button.

"In case it wasn't already obvious, you're invited back to my place for part two of our sleepover. We have some unfinished business, and I've been thinking of creative uses for that peach cobbler syrup." Quinn smirked.

"Ooh...not fair." He tugged her onto the elevator once the door opened and pushed the button for the fifth floor. "You're not the one who'll have to hide a raging hard-on from his entire family."

He backed her up against the elevator wall and kissed her, both of them trying not to spill their coffee. They got off on the fifth floor and he pulled her aside before they entered a set of secure doors. "Before we walk through those doors, you need to understand what you're getting yourself into," he said ominously.

"Okay," she said apprehensively. "Let's hear it."

He drank most of his cooled coffee then discarded the cup.

"My brothers will tease us mercilessly. My sister will try to push us down the aisle. And my mother will start dropping hints about grandchildren in a month or two, tops."

"You're exaggerating, Max." Quinn laughed, relieved. "Besides, I adore your family, and I'm prepared for whatever they dish out, as long as we're in this together."

"Don't say I didn't warn you." Max kissed her, then pulled away. He stared at her for a moment, a blissful smile animating his face. "By the way, not a proposal, but if I haven't already made it clear, I have every intention of marrying you, Quinn Bazemore."

"You'd better." She grinned. "Otherwise, good luck explaining to some woman why my initials are inked on your chest. *Awkward*."

"Good point, and that reminds me, we need to talk about which of my favorite poems you should incorporate in your tattoo," he teased, barely able to restrain his grin.

The two of them broke into laughter as they walked through the doors and into a private family waiting room, hand in hand.

Iris's brows furrowed with confusion and she whispered loudly to Duke, "I thought Quinn was Cole's girlfriend."

His father responded, "I think Cole did, too."

Cole shot them both a death stare and shook his head. "No one in this family ever listens to me."

He stood and hugged Quinn, then he shook his

brother's hand. They'd been making more of an effort to get along since Quinn had been spending time with both of them. "About time you two knuckleheads figured this out. And absolutely no pressure, but it would be nice to have someone else in this family besides Zora who actually gets me."

"I thought you said Zora would be the one pushing us down the aisle," Quinn whispered to Max loudly.

Zora bounded out of her chair and launched herself at Max, hugging him and then Quinn. "We can tag team the whole wedding thing," she said to Cole.

Max and Quinn settled into chairs next to each other amid the questions and excitement of his family. They were all inquisitive and teasing, but also warm and welcoming, making her feel like she was already one of their own.

Maybe she and Max had taken the long route to get here, but she was exactly where she'd always wanted to be.

* * * * *

One by one,
the Abbots are falling
for that special someone.
Now it's Zora's turn...

Don't miss the next
installment in
The Bourbon Brothers saga
by Reese Ryan!

Available February 2021
exclusively from
Harlequin Desire.